TIME
BOMB

TIME BOMB

BY **JOELLE CHARBONNEAU**

Houghton Mifflin Harcourt

BOSTON   NEW YORK

The text was set in Adobe Garamond Pro.

Library of Congress Cataloging-in-Publication Data
Names: Charbonneau, Joelle, author.
Title: Time bomb / by Joelle Charbonneau.
Description: Boston ; New York : Houghton Mifflin Harcourt, [2018] |
Summary: "Six students are trapped in their school after a bomb goes off, and must fight to survive while discovering who among them is the bomber." — Provided by publisher.
Identifiers: LCCN 2017006799 | ISBN 9780544416703
Subjects: | CYAC: Bombings — Fiction. | High schools — Fiction. | Schools — Fiction. | Emotional problems — Fiction. | Family problems — Fiction.
Classification: LCC PZ7.C37354 Tim 2018 | DDC [Fic] — dc23
LC record available at https://lccn.loc.gov/2017006799

Manufactured in the United States of America
DOC 10 9 8 7 6 5 4 3 2 1
4500697712

TO THE STUDENTS AND TEACHERS OF FENTON HIGH SCHOOL —
YOU TAUGHT ME FIRST IMPRESSIONS ARE NEVER
AS IMPORTANT AS WHAT COMES AFTER.

Nobody is the villain in their own story.

—George R.R. Martin

1:51 P.M.

"DON'T FIGHT," CAS SAID from the doorway that Frankie and Z had just disappeared through. Tears glistened in her eyes. "Can we turn the radio back on? Maybe they'll tell us help is finally coming."

Rashid clicked on the radio before heading over to help Tad. There was the buzz of static, then the announcer telling everyone that the firefighters were making progress. The fire was contained to the west side, and they hoped to have it out soon.

"With one person of interest being questioned, authorities are now working to find another individual they have confirmed is involved in this terrible bombing. A source confirms that the individual is one of the students trapped on the second floor of the school. With four bombs having already gone off, there appears to be one explosive device still inside the school that could detonate at any time."

Another bomb was ready to go off, and the bomber was one of *them*.

EARLIER THAT DAY . . .
8:35 A.M.

DIANA

— CHAPTER 1 —

ALL YOU HAD TO DO was smile and wear the right clothes, and everyone would think you were special. If you appeared successful, people would automatically assume you were successful. Her parents believed that. Her father had built a career on it. They wanted her to believe it.

Diana hated that she did.

"Perception is everything, Diana," her stepmother said so often that Diana wanted to scream. But screaming wasn't presentable. And, boy, did it make the wrong impression. This made screaming at the top of her lungs very tempting.

"Always take care to make the correct choice, Diana," her stepmother said over and over again. "Everything you do is important and reflects on your father and the positions he takes. And think about what your father's opponents would claim if you don't do well in school or become a leader in the activities you're in. They'll wonder how serious your father is about education if his own daughter doesn't do well in school. The other side is always looking for a reason to point fingers and show that your father isn't worthy of his position. That *we* aren't worthy. So you can't allow your grades or your attention to detail to slide, or you'll hurt your father and, worse, you'll hurt the work he's trying to do."

Diana looked down at the clothes she'd chosen for the day. After sixteen years, she knew exactly what details would be noticed and what people would think when they saw her.

Stylish white jeans. A tasteful pink top. But nothing too expensive, because that made people jealous. Nothing too tight, because that gave people the wrong idea. And no wrinkles. Wrinkles made people think you were lazy. No one trusts a person who is lazy. To get what you wanted in life, you must inspire trust—even if you intended to break it.

Her father inspired trust with his perfectly tailored suits that were made less stuffy because he never wore a tie and always left the collar open.

Folksy. Friendly. Everyone's idea of the perfect dad and former army-communications specialist who always puts his family and country first. At least that's what people must have thought, because he got elected. He was working hard to make sure he got to keep his job for another term, and it was their family's job—Diana's job—to make sure she didn't do anything wrong that could make voters question whether they wanted him back in office.

No pressure there.

"Katherine?" she yelled, knowing how much her stepmother hated raised voices. No response. *She must have already gone downstairs. Dad would be in meetings already.* Diana bit her lip as she reached for the gold studs Katherine gave her for her sixteenth birthday, then added the gold-cross necklace that had technically been from her father. She'd pretended not to notice when one of his aides handed him the box that he'd clearly been unaware of up until that moment.

"Little touches make all the difference," Katherine insisted. "People notice the details."

Yes, they did, Diana thought as she reached into her jewelry box and pulled out the ratty friendship bracelet she'd made for herself years ago, wishing she'd had someone to give it to and to get one in return from. No one ever assumed the popular girl needed to be given a gift. No one thought about whether the popular girl was lonely when she went home. Everyone assumed the popular girl had a million friends and a family who supported her.

Diana walked to her mirror and checked her makeup. Just enough to make her blue eyes look bigger. Nothing more, or people might question whether she was a good girl. And she was supposed to be a good girl. She ticked off her stepmother's checklist one by one.

Good shoes.

A nice home.

Top grades.

Smart, respectable family tree.

Perfect manners.

All signs of a strong, well-brought-up girl. A girl everyone claimed to know from school. One parents and teachers pointed to as an example to others. One who had been taught to calculate her appearance and demeanor down to the plain red color of her cell-phone case. One who was determined to use it all to show everyone that it was foolish to trust what someone wanted you to see.

Perfect.

And if she didn't want to ruin her perfect image, Diana would have to get moving. Tardiness was not acceptable for a girl who was supposed to be without flaws. Tardiness implied a lack of respect for other people's time.

Glancing at her watch, she shook her head and hurried downstairs to find her stepmother so she could get a ride to school for the yearbook meeting.

"Katherine?" she called.

No answer. *Huh.* Well, Katherine was probably in the backyard making sure the staff had polished the patio furniture to a shine so that guests could be invited back to the house after the event tonight.

"Katherine?"

"Your mother went out."

"What?" She turned and spotted her father standing next to the porch swing with his cell phone pressed to his ear. Since there was no point in correcting him about Katherine's relationship to her, she simply asked, "Where?"

He put up a hand to quiet her. "Yes, I'm here, and yes, I understand there's been some pushback, but I can't step back from the bill, or I'll get hammered. The press will smell blood and it'll be over, and we all know I'm right on this. I just need one thing to tip in my favor. You have to trust me on this."

Diana started to speak again, but before she could get a word out, her father turned his back and nodded. She would have to get in line for his attention.

"Yes. I'll make that distinction tonight, and don't worry. The event will be the perfect place to highlight the positive points in the bill and to take charge of the conversation. If you have other things you want to talk about, I'll be at the office in a half-hour. Good speaking with you, too, Tim. I appreciate your dedication. We're going to turn things around." Finally he hung up and turned toward her.

He was wearing perfectly pressed khakis and a red polo shirt under a deep blue sports coat—*relaxed authority* was what her stepmother called the look. But despite the clothes, Diana didn't think her father appeared relaxed.

"That was Tim?"

Her father nodded. "He's worried about the negative press my Safety Through Education bill is getting."

Tim hadn't been on her father's staff as long as the others, but he was smart and perceptive, which is why her father's chief of staff hired him right out of graduate school. And even though he was younger than the rest of the staff, Diana knew Tim was right to be worried about her father's bill. The press was calling it an invasion of privacy. The law would require that students and teachers inform the administration if they thought someone in the school might be interested in doing harm to students, teachers, or school property. Any students reported would then have to hand over their passwords to social media and email accounts or face suspension and a potential investigation by federal authorities. Those who didn't report suspicions before a harmful event could be charged with aiding and abetting.

Her father believed the law would turn everything in the country around and would finally do what no other laws had been able to do—make things safer. Any students interested in causing trouble would think twice about it if they knew their friends and teachers were watching them and ready to act on any suspicious activity. And by catching and circumventing threatening behavior early, there was a good chance of diverting those students toward a more positive path. Her father was certain that taking action in the schools and the education system was the best way of changing the escalating pattern of violence in the country.

"Was there another bad story in the press?" Diana asked. Not everyone agreed with her father's thoughts on how to keep the country safe. Since the unveiling of the bill, there had been phone calls and mail and huge editorials about invasion of privacy and people's differing definitions of what a "threat" to society actually was. Diana had even gotten hate mail for her father's idea. When she had tried to talk to her father about it, he had just told her to give the mail to Tim and ignore it. That everything would work out. But when Tim had sat with her and listened to her talk about the threats she'd gotten and how people made a point of telling her they were going to vote her father out of office, Tim had admitted the backlash was concerning. If the tide of bad press and angry editorials about the potential law continued, they both agreed that it would be sunk before it ever had a chance to be tested. And her father's career—one she had been told was necessary to make the world better—would be sunk along with it.

Was it any wonder Tim wanted to pull out all the stops to make sure her father's event tonight got the press's attention, or that she was willing to do whatever it took to help? It was nice to have someone finally realize that she was capable of helping, and to finally listen to her when she had an idea. And Tim had said he was glad he could run ideas by someone without having to worry about her telling the senator that his ideas were too radical or that he wasn't up to the job.

Her father shrugged and gave her his own practiced smile. "Some of my co-sponsors are wondering if we should shelve the idea for more study, but Tim has some polling that says retreating might do more harm than good. I'm not worried. Tim and the others have a plan to make this all come together."

"If you need me—"

Her father held up his hand as the phone rang. The phone was always ringing. "I'll catch this on my way to the office." He looked at Diana and gave her a tense smile. "Your mother left a note for you on the counter. You can help by making sure you're ready when she comes to pick you up. I need everything to be perfect if we're going to turn this around." Then, before she could say anything, her father put the phone to his ear and said, "Larry, I'm glad you called . . ." as he disappeared into the house.

Diana hurried after him, but he didn't bother to look back. A minute later, Diana heard the front door slam behind him as he left before she could remind him that she needed a ride. And when she read her stepmother's note, she knew she wasn't going to get one from her, either.

> *Diana dear,*
> *I'll be home to pick you up at four. Wear the blue satin dress hanging in your closet and leave your hair down. Please be on time. Tonight is very important to all of us.*
> *Katherine*

She stared at the letter.

Be on time.

Leave your hair down.

Tonight is important.

But, clearly, driving Diana to school today was not.

She turned the bracelet on her arm again, looked at her

stepmother's words one more time, hearing each of them ringing in her head along with all the other things she'd said over
the years.

"Keep your opinions to yourself, Diana." Because they
might differ from what she was supposed to think. And that
wasn't allowed.

"Remember that we're counting on you."

Yes. They were.

Diana headed back upstairs to the antique toy chest in the
corner of her room. Quickly, she dumped the decorative pillows
and extra blanket stacked on top onto the floor, then lifted the
lid. She pulled out two bags. In the side pocket of one of the
bags, she found the list she'd made for herself a few weeks ago
and put it in her pocket.

A quick glance at the clock told her she'd better get going or
she'd be late for the yearbook meeting. Yesterday she'd moved
the meeting to two hours earlier than originally scheduled. She
doubted anyone would be thrilled that she'd asked them to
change their plans simply to make them wait.

Diana turned, took one last look in the mirror and saw
what her family wanted her to be. What she had tried so hard
to pretend to be.

Perfect. Someone everyone expected to do the right thing
and no one would ever suspect of doing something wrong.

Good.

Booting up her computer, she sent a quick message to Tim,

telling him that she was going to school now. Then Diana carefully picked up her bags and headed downstairs and out the door. Her father thought the only contribution he needed from her was for her to nod and smile and look flawless — like their family was supposed to be. She was determined to prove him wrong.

9:52 A.M.

RASHID

— CHAPTER 2 —

"**WHY DO YOU** have to go to the school today?" his father asked, coming into the kitchen. Rashid had hoped to get out of the house before his father had gotten home from the hospital. So much for that idea. "Your classes do not start for another week."

Rashid hefted the bag he had slung over his shoulder and explained, "I need a new school ID, Father."

"What happened to your old one?" His father looked at him with a frown.

"I lost it when we were visiting with Sitto last month." Technically, that was true. Although Rashid knew his words implied that he had *accidentally* left his ID behind at his grandmother's in Palestine. "The office is open for new students to get IDs. I thought I should do it now instead of waiting until school starts."

His father nodded, then glanced at the kitchen clock. "Will you be back by the start of Dhuhr?"

"I don't think so."

"I can call and see if the office will be open during the afternoon. If you wait, we can pray together, and then maybe you can take your sister. It would be good for her to see the school without so many people. It'll help her get used to the idea of going there next year. You could introduce her to some of your friends."

His sister already knew most of his friends, since they either lived nearby or went to mosque together. The others . . .

His father thought he understood what it was like for Rashid at school, but he had no idea. He didn't listen. Or maybe Rashid's cousins in Palestine were right, and it was Rashid's fault he didn't completely fit in, because he did not know who he was or what he wanted.

A few years ago, he would have brought his sister with him to school. But that was then. Now . . . so much had changed. He was different. His sister certainly was, and his friends . . . They all still enjoyed the comics and building robots, which held their friendships together. But Rashid could tell there were other things—like the facial hair that he had started growing earlier than anyone else in his class, and the adherence to his faith that prevented him from shaving it—that were creating an invisible wall between them.

He bit back the anger that seemed harder and harder to keep hidden and respectfully said, "Next time. I don't know who will be there, and I don't want her to have a bad experience."

It was hard enough for Rashid to fit in, especially now. He didn't want to bring Arissa. The hijab made her stand out even more than his untrimmed beard did. But Arissa didn't seem to mind wearing it. More than once, she said that she liked the attention the hijab brought, and it helped her know exactly who her friends were. The hijab signaled who she was and that she was proud of her heritage. She said if people didn't like it, they could just get out of her way.

Rashid wondered if it wasn't easier for her because the hijab was so obvious and its meaning so clear. Since some of the other students chose to grow beards and mustaches, his own beard was sometimes interpreted as a personal choice instead of a mandate of faith. But it often raised questions he could see in people's eyes that never got spoken aloud — not even by his friends. If he had been braver, he might just have sat down and talked to his friends about it and helped them understand. Instead, he let the silences get longer.

Now he felt he had only one option open to him.

"I should probably go now so I don't have to stand in line all day," Rashid said, feeling the weight of the bag pulling on his shoulder. "I will pray at school." There were plenty of empty classrooms. Since it wasn't a school day, he wouldn't have to worry about people making fun of him washing in the bathroom first. "I'll be home as soon as I can."

His father smiled. "No need to rush. If you see people you know, you should spend time with them. You haven't had the chance to see any of your friends this summer. The best life has balance. Maybe while you're at school, you can see if there are any new clubs you'd like to join, although I still think you should take photos for the yearbook. The pictures you took this summer are very good."

"I'll look into it," Rashid said, knowing he wouldn't. He had other things to do. He just hoped his father would be able to understand.

"Good." His father patted him on the arm and frowned. "Why are you taking your school bag?"

Rashid smiled to hide his nerves. "I'm bringing some note-books and comic books and a couple of other things to put in my locker so I don't have to bring everything on the first day. I like having stuff to read in study hall."

He also read when his friends were late for lunch, to avoid drawing the attention of some of the football players, who liked to harass him.

"Using extra time for study is always good." His father patted him on the arm again. "Do you have your Koran?"

"No," Rashid said, shifting toward the door. "I'm leaving it here. I've got to go."

"Wait a second." His father disappeared out of the kitchen and returned holding a thick paperback that Rashid had no choice but to take. "You might be glad to have it at school with you."

Rashid forced himself to thank his father, but he couldn't meet his eyes as he walked out the door. He put the book in the bag and headed to school, still trying to decide if he was going to go through with his plan.

Was this really the time to draw the line in the sand?

He thought about the names he'd been called last year and how uncomfortable his non-Muslim friends looked when they pretended that they were all the same. That nothing had changed.

He wished nothing had changed. More than anything, he wanted to turn back the clock to before the beard and the suspicion it brought into focus. Things had already been hard then, but they had been better.

Hitching the bag so that the weight was better distributed, Rashid frowned and started walking faster. If he was going to change things, he had to do it today. He only hoped that he had the courage to do what needed to be done.

9:58 A.M.

Z

"YOU'RE KICKING ME OUT?" Sweat pricked Z's back and forehead. He should have had two more months. His mother had said they'd agreed. And now he was getting screwed.

Z turned his back on the landlord's son. He couldn't look at the satisfied smile on the jerk's pimply face without wanting to deck the guy. Z felt like hitting something—everything.

"Not exactly," Nick said. "I mean, I know my dad and your mom talked about trying to lower the rent over the summer to help you out, but my dad realized that if he changed the terms of the lease for *you,* he'd have to do it for everyone, and you know how that goes. It's not like my father *wants* to do this."

Sure he does, Z thought. *He just doesn't want to* say *he wants to boot the guy who's just lost his mother to cancer. That would make him have to admit he's a crappy person.* But that's what he was. All Nick's father knew was that a guaranteed rent check was dead and buried. It was time to find a new one, and to hell with anything else. Yeah—Z knew exactly how that went.

"I'm sure this is breaking your father's heart." Z clenched his fists and looked out the narrow window over the sink. If he closed his eyes, he could still see his mother standing there, washing dishes . . . when she had been well enough to do something that normal.

"Hey, don't be like that."

"Like what?" Z turned and stared at the guy. Nick straightened his shoulders but took a step back, tugging at the hem of his dirty T-shirt. "Your father made a promise to my dying mom, and two weeks after she's gone, he sends you to tell me he was just kidding."

Nick took another step back and swallowed hard. "He's really sorry about this."

"Sure he is." Everyone was sorry. Z was so tired of hearing everyone tell him how damn sorry they were. Only they weren't. But they would be. Soon. Very soon. Z unclenched his fists and turned back toward the off-white fridge that his mother had plastered with photographs. "Tell your dad not to beat himself up about it. It's no problem, *Nicky*," he added, yanking open the fridge. The cool air washed over him, helping to tamp down the anger he wanted to let break free. Despite the open windows, the apartment was sweltering.

"Hey, kid, if it was up to me, I would let you stay. I know things are tough. After everything that happened, this really sucks, but—"

"It's fine," Z said, grabbing a bottle of tap water out of the fridge. It wasn't fine. There was nothing fine about being told by a twenty-seven-year-old guy who lived in his parents' basement and had Cheetos stains on his T-shirt that you had to clear out in three weeks. *Adios, boy. Don't let the door hit your long-haired, tattooed self on the way out.*

"Look, my father would like to be able to let you stay. He really liked your mom. She was a nice lady."

"Yeah." Z closed the fridge and looked at the photo of his mother's happy, healthy face pressed next to his five-year-old chocolate-coated one. "She was great."

Was.

He swallowed hard while, behind him, Nick Mansanelli said, "I could talk to my dad about having you do some work on our cars in exchange for staying in their attic. It's not the best place, but it would give you some time to sort out whatever it is you're going to do next. I'm sure you could use the—"

"No need." Z would rather sleep in a ditch than become slave labor for anyone. He uncapped the cold water and took a drink. "Tell your dad pretty soon he won't have to worry about dealing with me ever again."

Nick took another step back and rubbed his hand against the back of his neck as he looked around. "Can I . . . you know . . . help you do anything? Do you need some boxes or tape?" Nick turned toward the living room and nodded. "You got a lot of stuff to pack up around here. Why don't I—"

"No." Before Nick could step into the hallway that led to the bedrooms, Z stalked forward and blocked him. "I don't need your help." Z didn't need anyone.

Nick frowned. "Are you sure? I mean, it's no prob—"

"I'm sure," Z said as the phone in his back pocket chimed. He pulled it out and looked down at the display.

YOU OK? DID YOU HEAR FROM YOUR UNCLE IN CALIFORNIA? I'M WORRIED ABOUT YOU. PLEASE TALK TO ME.

Kaitlin.

Of all the people who said they wanted to help, she actually did. But there wasn't much more she could do or say. She kept telling him it was okay to be angry. That it would get better if he just gave it time. They all warned him about making decisions too fast. Urged him to give the relatives he barely remembered a chance to reach out. He had to give things time.

But time wasn't going to change the fact that his mother was dead and that everything sucked.

Kaitlin had been there for him when everyone else had bailed. Extended family. Neighbors. Teachers. He'd tried to tell her to get lost when she followed him out of the school after he'd been in detention. But she dogged him all the way to the parking lot and insisted he give her a ride home. Her mother was a nurse at the hospital where his mother got treatments. It wasn't as if he was going to say no, but that didn't mean he was going to talk to her. Which was probably what Kaitlin wanted, since she had plenty to say. Kaitlin had been determined to be his friend, even when he didn't want her to be. Even when he cut school more than he bothered to go. If it hadn't been for her, he wasn't sure he would have made it this far.

And now he was going to cut her loose before he dragged her down. She deserved better.

Z shoved the phone into his pocket and looked back at Nick.

"Look," Z said with a deliberate sigh. "If that's all you came here for, I've got to get going. There's a teacher I have to talk to at school, and I don't want to miss him."

Nick slapped Z on the shoulder. The universal sign for *I want you to think I've got your back, even though I plan on screwing you the first chance I get.* "Hey, no problem. I just came by to see how you were doing and make sure you didn't need anything before—"

Before you chucked me to the curb. Z again clenched his hands into fists at his side, and Nick backed up a step.

Finally, the guy turned toward the front door and said, "Hey, make sure to take care of yourself. And give them hell at that school. I never liked it much anyway."

At last, one thing they could agree on.

Z chugged the water, then headed down the hall toward his room to grab his father's old army duffle and the letter that had arrived last week. His cell phone chimed as he was slinging the bag onto his shoulders, but he ignored it. He had things to do.

In the kitchen, he grabbed the picture of him and Mom and slid it next to his phone. He then walked out of the apartment. No need to lock the door. If someone wanted to clear the rest out, let them. He was going to school, and he wasn't coming back.

10:03 A.M.

TAD

– CHAPTER 4 –

TAD GLANCED DOWN at his phone to see if he just missed hearing the text coming in.

Nothing.

> HEY. JUST CHECKING TO SEE IF YOU WANTED TO HANG TODAY, SINCE WE DON'T HAVE PRACTICE. NOT SURE IF MY LAST MESSAGE WENT THROUGH.

He hit SEND and threw his phone down on his bed before throwing himself down next to it. Of course the message went through yesterday, as had all the others he'd sent and hadn't gotten a response to since football practice started a few weeks ago.

Still, he kept sending them. He let himself hope that maybe he'd get one in response — as he had for the dozens they'd shared before suddenly everything had changed.

Stupid. Sixteen and in love with a guy who didn't return

his texts and avoided the hell out of him at football practice. Like Tad was going to hold his hand or pat his ass in front of the other guys and let everyone know they'd hooked up this summer. He still wasn't sure how it happened. It was almost like some B-movie script. Tad had turned and had seen Frankie watching him. That one look changed everything. Normally, Tad left parties early, but that look during that Fourth of July party made him stick around long after everyone else had gone. He hadn't expected anything. He'd just wanted to hang. After all, the guy had bagged half the cheerleaders and had even dated Miss Perfect Rich Girl, Diana Sanford. Hell, he'd never given any sign that he was gay or that he was attracted to anyone other than white girls.

That night, they'd just talked—about the team and the upcoming season and what the two of them wanted out of life beyond high school. Nothing earth-shattering. Just . . . talk.

The next day, Tad got a text asking if they could meet up and practice running some plays—only the final play that day didn't involve throwing the football. Tad could still feel the way their hands brushed. At first, Tad thought it was accidental. Then it happened again, with a shy smile. And he knew they both were interested in being more than friends.

Tad rolled over and reached for his phone. The display remained dark. How hard was it to return a text? Or to say, *Hey, I'm not sure I'm up for this relationship.* Yeah, the conversation would suck, but at least there wouldn't be this void. There wouldn't be seeds of hope and resentment growing in the silence. There wouldn't be the desire to see the phone light up with the message telling him that he was worth paying attention to. That there was nothing to be ashamed of.

Music, if anyone could call the crap his brother liked to listen to that, suddenly shook the walls.

Ugh. Tad grabbed the football from the floor and sent it flying against the wall, hoping his brother would get the hint.

Sam cranked the music louder, if that was possible. *Damn him.*

Tad stormed into the hall and banged on his brother's door. The decibel level went up again. He pounded on the door with both hands and yelled, "Turn that crap down!"

Suddenly the door flew open. The volume level was now earsplitting.

"What do you want?" Tad's older brother stood in the doorway with his guitar slung around his neck and a scowl on his face. They were only a year apart in age but eons apart in everything else.

"What do you think I want?" Tad asked, rolling his eyes. "I want you to turn that noise down."

Sam shook his head and crossed his arms. "Not in this lifetime. You're supposed to be at practice, which means I get to play my music as loud as I want. That's the deal."

A deal Sam conveniently ignored whenever he felt like it, and their mother, who brokered the compromise in the first place, always let Sam get away with it. If Dad were around, it might be different. Or maybe if Tad were different . . .

"I don't have practice today."

"That's not my problem." Sam smiled. "This is my time. You can stay or you can go, and if you have an issue with that, feel free to take it up with Mom. She and her friends just came in."

"Sam, could you cut me a break this once?" Tad asked. "Things suck right now, and I just need to be able to think without my head feeling like it's going to explode."

Sam leaned against the doorjamb as the screeching song ended and a slower but equally loud ballad began. "Having trouble with the team or with your boyfriend?"

Tad stiffened. "I don't have a boyfriend."

He'd come out to his family a few months ago, but his mother still hadn't told any of her well-meaning friends, who thought Tad would make a great boyfriend for one of their daughters or nieces. Just thinking about it made his head hurt worse.

Sam laughed. "Sure thing."

"I don't."

"You forget that it isn't just music that can be heard through these walls. I might not have caught everything you were saying on those late-night calls a few weeks ago, but it was enough to guess what was going on."

"I was just talking to a friend. No big deal." Tad jammed his phone into his pocket.

Sam shrugged and adjusted the guitar strap on his neck. "Well, this is no big deal either." The door slammed in Tad's face, and the lock clicked into place.

No big surprise there.

His brother never used to lock his door or avoid him this way.

His mother's friends didn't used to bring their daughters over quite so much.

If his father were here, he'd tell Tad to hang in there. That everyone would settle in with time. That people would get over it.

Only they never did.

The phone in his hand vibrated, and he hated how his heart jumped, then fell as he looked at the screen and saw it was from Jimmy, the team's center.

TEAM PARTY AT LAKE TODAY. MEET AT MY HOUSE AT NOON. NO ONE IS TO GO NEAR THE SCHOOL OR JV PRACTICE TODAY. CAPTAIN'S ORDERS.

Don't go near the school. Captain's orders. And when their captain gave an order, most of the team fell in line, because Frankie was the guy no one crossed without getting benched in favor of a player Coach had suddenly realized was better. Tad always fell in line. He didn't like to make waves because, he told himself, he'd already made waves by being who he was: Not black. Not white. And on top of that, not straight. So he shouldn't rock the boat. He should just be grateful when people acted normal around him.

Well, screw that.

Tad looked down at the text message again.

After being pushed aside for weeks, he knew he was done pretending everything was just fine. Nothing was fine, and he was done taking orders. He was done being ignored.

The bass of his brother's music pulsing in his chest, Tad went back to his room and grabbed his gym bag. Locking his door, he went through everything in the bag, just to make sure he hadn't forgotten anything.

Everything on the list he'd made was there. Ready. Today he was going to insist on being noticed. No more sitting around, waiting for someone else to take action.

He lifted the bag onto his shoulder, then headed down the hall, determined to act as if there was nothing special going on. *Nothing to see here, kids.* Just a guy going about his business like it was any other day. No big statements to make. No lives to change. And it wouldn't be just his life that changed if he went through with this.

Tad banged on Sam's door again as he passed by. Sam cranked up the music again. Tad punched on the door one more time, then started out, wondering what his brother would think about his plan.

Oh, hell. He'd forgotten about his mother and her friends in the kitchen.

"The money is good, but if Dan has to keep traveling like

this, I'm going to lose what little is left of my mind. I can't keep doing all this alone. Raising boys is complicated."

Tad went completely still.

"Well, Dan is going to have to tell them he has kids at home and can't be away as much."

His mother's voice floated down the hall. He thought he could make out Mrs. O'Neil's voice, too, and that of Mrs. O'Neil's daughter, Jasmine. *Ugh.*

"I swear his boss looks at the pictures of the boys and assumes they aren't his. Sometimes I wonder if he thinks he's doing Dan a favor by having him go on all these out-of-town trips. If we didn't have bills to pay, I'd give him a piece of my mind."

Mrs. O'Neil said something that Tad couldn't hear. But his mother was perfectly clear when she said, "Jasmine, honey, why don't you go knock on Tad's door and see if he's around? His practice got canceled today, and I'm sure he's looking for something to do."

"That's a wonderful idea, Jas." Mrs. O'Neil jumped on top of that in a way that said she and Tad's mother had planned the idea in advance. "The two of you should go see a movie. Why don't you go see if he wants to?"

Damn. He needed to get out of here . . . fast.

"You know where his room is, right?" Tad's mother asked as a chair scraped against the kitchen tile.

Tad took that as his cue to bolt for the door, while Mrs. O'Neil said something about his mother being so lucky. That Tad and Sam were both such handsome boys.

Tad hurried onto the front walk and down the street, hoping his brother's crappy music covered the sound of his leaving. He'd reached the end of the block when he got a text from his mother.

WHERE ARE YOU? JASMINE IS HERE AND THOUGHT YOU MIGHT LIKE TO SEE A MOVIE.

No. No, I wouldn't.

He walked faster toward the school, more determined than when he'd left. How many times had he told his mother to stop meddling in his life? She couldn't see anything other than her own point of view — just like everyone else. Words were useless. They were ignored. Well, he was done being ignored.

Since words didn't seem to change anything, it was time to take action. People might want to bury their heads in the sand, but he wasn't going to give them that option. Not anymore. They were going to take notice whether they wanted to or not.

No more just waiting for change. He had waited long enough. Tried talking long enough.

Well, the time for talking was over, and the time for doing was here. He was going to be noticed. He wasn't going to be turned away anymore. Was he scared? Hell, yeah. But sometimes the only way to change something was to break it first.

10:13 A.M.

CAS

— CHAPTER 5 —

"TODAY WOULD HAVE BEEN a great riding day. Don't you think?"

"Sure, Mom." If a person liked riding horses. Cas gave her mom a smile, then looked out the car's window. The sun was shining. The sky was blue, with white puffy clouds, but she would have been just as terrible and looked just as stupid on horseback in the sunshine as in the drizzle or the dark. Her mother knew that, but she liked to pretend Cas was something other than what she was. She kept imagining that Cas would someday be like the rest of them. Just as Cas's father wanted. Just as everyone seemed to want.

Normal.

Popular.

Someone her family could be proud of. Because she wasn't good enough now. And she was pretty sure no matter what she did, she never would be.

"You know, we could always go back." Mom almost sang the idea, and Cas cringed. "There're still nine days until school starts for all of you. We could ditch your dad, and the rest of us could go back until then. Grammy and Pop-Pop would love it, and your brothers and sisters would be over the moon, especially Midge."

Her littlest sister, Midge, had fallen in love with a kitten and cried for hours after they'd left the farm. If they went back, the kid would end up crying all over again. It didn't seem fair to promise Midge happiness only to keep taking it away. Cas knew how that felt. She didn't want her sister to end up like her.

When Cas didn't respond, her mother said, "Well, think about it. I'll talk to your father and let him know we might head back for a couple days. Once you fix your schedule today, we won't have anything to do until school starts. We've already been back-to-school shopping, right?" Mom reached over and adjusted the gauzy, decorative silver-and-black scarf she'd insisted on looping around Cas's neck this morning, then looked back toward the road. "It's all going to be great. You'll see."

Or she wouldn't.

Her mother always said things would be great. Cas used to believe her, but it had turned out that was stupid, because it was never true. Not now. Not when they moved here a year ago. Everyone had said it was for her father's job, but they all knew differently.

It'll be closer to Grammy and Pop-Pop's farm. You'll get to start fresh and make new friends. Everything is going to be so much better, Cas. If you just try, it'll all be great.

Cas looked out the window again, twisted a lock of her long

black hair around her fingers, and studied the school in the distance. She was glad she didn't feel like running away or hiding when she looked at it anymore. Three stories of brick and steel and crappy people who judged everything because they thought they knew so much. They thought they understood all there was to know just by looking at her. They thought they knew her.

They didn't. They didn't know anything. No one did anymore.

"You're so quiet, Cas." Her mother glanced away from the road and over at her. "You know, we can always do homeschooling if you want. Or there's the Catholic school you could go to, if you don't want to come back here. I know your father and Dr. Nepali think you'll be fine, but I want you to know you have options. After everything that happened, it's okay that it takes time for you to feel all-the-way better, and if you want—"

"No." Cas shook her head and mimicked her mother's upbeat tone as she said, "Dad and Dr. Nepali are right. What happened is in the past. It happened somewhere else, and it's not like I can change it, anyway. The only thing I can change is myself. I have to move on."

Sneers in the hallway. Being tripped. Being mocked as she was pushed down. Friends scared to stand up for her. Friends too scared of people making fun of them or worse if they decided to stay friends. The desire for everything to go away. To just end it all because of something that had started as words on a screen. Or maybe it had started before, and Cas hadn't noticed.

"Well, you still have time to change your mind. A new school is always an option."

Not for her. After months of trying to make herself believe it would get better, Cas had made up her mind. For the first time in what seemed like forever, she was able to really focus and think about what she wanted. A new school wouldn't change anything, because it couldn't change what had happened. And it couldn't change her.

She glanced behind her at the bag she'd stashed in the back seat as her mother pulled the SUV to a stop at the curb at the base of the dozens of steps that led to the main entrance.

"I can come in with you if you want. My errands can wait. Honey, how about I come in with you?"

Cas looked at her mom and for a moment wanted to say yes. She wanted to go back to the time when she could say yes and she and her mother would laugh at everything. But there was no going back.

"Once I get my schedule changed, I'm going to go practice for a while." Cas opened the car door before her mother could insist on escorting Cas inside. "You don't need to come in. Everything is going to be fine now. It's like Dad said, I have to take charge of my life and stop whining about being unhappy. Whining won't get me anywhere. I have to choose to change things."

"Your father loves you, Cas," Mom said as Cas opened the back door and grabbed the large turquoise bag off the seat. "He's worried. You know how he gets when he's worried."

Worried was the wrong word. *Disappointed* was the right one. Cas should know. He'd been disappointed in her for longer than she probably knew.

"Well, I'm going to make sure he doesn't have to worry anymore. I promise," Cas said, shoving the door closed and turning toward the school that last year her father had assured her would make everything better.

A school with more than three thousand students will give you lots of options, Cassandra. With that many students, you'll find people you have things in common with. No one will know anything about what happened before, so it should be easy for you to find friends. Just avoid anyone you don't get along with, and everything will be different than it was before.

She looked up at the large staircases on either side of the incline that led to the main entrance above and remembered how she'd clung to her father's words. How she'd looked at the sprawling brick-and-cement three-story building from the bottom of the steps with its narrow, shining glass windows and at the brand-new auditorium with its bright marquees welcoming everyone the first day of class. She'd felt a spurt of hope. She'd made herself believe that everything would magically be better. That she'd be better.

"I have my phone on in case you need me. I'll be back soon,"

Cas's mother called. Cas nodded and tried not to care when her mother added, "I love you."

"Me too, Mom," Cas said, straightening her blue shirt. Then she hitched the bag on her shoulder and started walking toward the red-brick stairs that led up to the school that had been nothing but a disappointment. If she'd thought things would be any different at the smaller Catholic school her mother had been pushing her to consider, Cas would have tried it. But she'd learned that big school or little school didn't make any difference. Nothing ever changed. It didn't matter what she wore or how she acted or if she lost weight. People always judged.

Well, the girls who made snide comments about her clothes and the boys who laughed at her weight could have their opinions. She had opinions too. Each time she climbed on one of those stupid horses and ate a freaking carrot to make her father nod with approval, she thought about how she would never please anyone. No matter what she said or what she wore or how hard she tried. They had already decided she wasn't good enough. And she was done trying to gain the approval of people who thought they could make themselves feel better by pushing her and then kicking her when she was down.

Cas pulled the stupid scarf from around her neck, jammed it into her bag, and yanked open one of the glass doors.

She was done with it all.

10:23 A.M.

FRANKIE

– CHAPTER 6 –

"HEY, KIDDO." Frankie ruffled his sister's curly blond hair and snagged a banana from the basket in the center of the table.

She rolled her eyes. "I just about gave you up for dead. Mom already did. She left fifteen minutes ago to help set up for youth group tonight. She said if you woke up before dinnertime to let you know."

"Hey, I have to sleep now while I can. We'll both be getting up at six a.m. next week." He stopped peeling the banana. "Oh, wait. You'll have to get up earlier, since you have to catch the bus, because that's what freshmen do."

Frankie dodged the napkin she threw at him and grinned as she called him a jerk. "I'm not a jerk. I'm a junior, which means I've done the dorky freshman thing. Now it's your turn, and I cannot wait to make some popcorn, watch the show, and laugh." He picked up the napkin, balled it, and pitched it into the trashcan. *Nothing but net.*

"You're such a showoff."

"Dad says that it would be a sin against God for a person not to use the skill he or she was born with. And I think we can both agree that I have skills."

Bianca rolled her eyes, and Frankie laughed as he headed to the fridge to grab a soda.

"So which of those mad skills are you planning to use today?" Bianca asked. "Your fierce gluttony or your well-developed sloth?"

"I think sloth has already been accounted for, and gluttony is coming up next." He shoved the banana in his mouth. His sister let out an *eww* and swatted at him the way he knew she would. After he'd chased down the banana with Mountain Dew, he added, "But if you need the rest of the agenda for your report to Mom, I've got practice."

"Wait." His sister's brown eyes narrowed. "I thought today's practice was canceled because you won some stupid bet."

"You are correct, although not about the bet being stupid." It had been smart and calculated. Frankie had made a bet that Coach couldn't resist.

"As a result of my superior intellect and outstanding athletic prowess, varsity football practice was canceled for the day. JV, however, is still meeting, because they don't have a leader with my vision and sense of purpose."

"And you've decided your new purpose will be to crash their practice and show off your overrated athletic skills? Or are you going to sit in the bleachers and laugh your ass off as they trip all over themselves trying to impress you?"

"Neither." Although both were totally viable options. "We're going for the prize behind door number three."

He chugged his soda and grabbed his car keys from the hook by the door. A couple of stops to pick up the rest of the things he needed, and everything would be ready to go.

"You're going to prank the JV. You are, aren't you?"

He turned and was struck by how tall Bianca had gotten. Not close to his six feet two, but taller than Mom. And she did a good impression of Mom, with the way her head was cocked to the side as if trying to decide whether she should finally call him on his crap. Mom never did, but Bianca wasn't as willing to let him slide. If she kept up that no-BS mentality, his sister would survive high school without a problem.

But that didn't mean he wasn't going to try to snow her. With a smile, he said, "According to the *Athletic Code of Conduct Handbook,* hazing is not acceptable behavior at Hallwood High School."

"And still somehow when you were a freshman, you ended up with shaving cream in your helmet and cayenne pepper on your jockstrap."

Those were the days. Okay, maybe not the burning sensation that plagued him for days, but the rest. Well, everything seemed easier when he was a freshman. Now . . . well, that was then. This was now.

He turned and headed down the hall.

"Come on, Frankie. Tell me. What are you guys going to do to the JV?" She followed him into the garage. When he didn't tell, she said, "Fine. Maybe I'll just have to come down to the school so I can see for myself."

"No." His head snapped toward Bianca. "You're not coming to school. Not today."

"You might be the almighty captain of the football team, but you don't own the place. I can go wherever the hell I want, and as it turns out, a lot of freshman will be getting new IDs today. So I might want to go and hang out with some of my friends who still have to get theirs."

"You're not interested in seeing your friends. All you're trying to do is shove yourself into my life. Isn't it enough that we're already attending the same school and going to the same church group? Can't a guy do anything without his family spying on him?"

Bianca crossed her arms in front of her chest and raised her chin the way she used to do when she was six and was about to cry. Which was just perfect. His sister needed to learn to let things go. She'd be happier if she did. Of course, he probably wasn't one to give advice on that front. Especially not when he considered what his plans were for today.

His phone chimed, and he glanced down at the text.

"I just want to see what you're doing," his sister said quietly, making him feel like a total jerk. "It's not like I'm spying or that I'm going to tell Mom or Dad."

"Look," he said, checking the text again, then the clock on his phone. He had to get going if he was going to make his plans fly. "The guys and I are just going to have a little fun.

We're not going to get caught, because we know what we're do-ing." And even if he did get caught, nothing would probably happen. Because no one would dare sideline the all-American star football and baseball player. Not if it meant there was a chance they'd lose a game. "But if you're seen at the school, you'll probably be asked if you saw anything. Then you'll either have to rat us out and commit social suicide before even starting high school or you'll end up in detention for forever. I wouldn't recommend either. Okay?" When Bianca didn't look as if she was going to stand down, he pushed harder. "Bianca, I'm trying to protect you. Brothers do that, even for their annoying fresh-man sisters."

"Fine." Bianca unfolded her arms and tucked her hands in her back pockets with a shrug. She tried to pretend she was unyielding, but he could see she was smiling, which made the tension in him ease. He liked when his sister thought of him as one of the good guys . . . even if he knew he'd done things that might make her question it.

Frankie grinned wider when his sister added, "But I want to hear all about it later."

"I don't think you have to worry about that."

People would notice, and no one would call him out. Because he had an arm that won games. What could possibly be more important than that?

Frankie slid behind the wheel of the old white Mustang his dad had given him when he'd become the varsity's starting quarterback. It had been accompanied by the words *Just don't think you can spend all your time in the back seat with your girl-friend. You still have work to do.*

Of course I do, Frankie thought now as he cranked the engine to life. Nothing was ever good enough. A winner always had to do more.

He started to back out but stopped and rolled down the window as he spotted his sister going back into the house. "Hey, Bianca. I'm not kidding. Stay away from school today. Promise me."

"Yeah. Yeah. I promise." And she slammed the door shut.

Good. He picked up his phone and read a new text that had just come in. He answered the second one and looked at the first one a long time before shaking his head and putting the phone down. Then he put the car in reverse and hit the gas. It was time to get this show on the road.

10:43 A.M.

RASHID

−CHAPTER 7 −

THERE WAS ALREADY a line for new student identification cards for students who had been unable to get them at the end of school last year or had lost them.

The main office door, located in the middle of the two-story-tall atrium under the purple-and-yellow painted signs that said MIGHTY TROJANS, was closed. The lights were on in the office, but whoever was in charge of processing IDs hadn't started yet, which meant that everyone had to wait outside in the atrium or somewhere else nearby. A couple of kids were standing near the door. One girl from last year's chemistry class smiled and nodded. Rashid nodded back but didn't walk over to join her, instead he looked around at the others who were waiting. Some were sitting on the floor in the foyer, and he could see a bunch more camping out past the double doors that officially led to the rest of the school.

Rashid looked at his watch, then counted the students outside the office doors and the ones in the front hall stationed near the media center. There were twenty who had arrived before he had — none were from his group of friends. He'd perform Dhuhr early, as he often did when school was in session, then get in line after he was done.

He let a dark-haired girl holding a blue bag and a clarinet case walk through the doors in front of him, then headed into the main front hall. The girl turned right — toward the fine arts wing. Rashid went left, past the media-center doors. The closest bathrooms were to the right of the media center, but there were too many people hanging out in that direction. He wasn't sure he'd have the courage to follow through with what he'd come here to do if he had to look at all of them as he passed by. Besides, it would be easier to pray in one of the classrooms upstairs, where there were fewer people.

A couple of girls hurried in his direction, their shoes squeaking against the light-gray tile. Rashid stepped to the side to avoid them and felt his bag bump into something on the other side.

"Um . . . excuse me?" a girl snapped.

"I'm sorry," Rashid automatically said as he pulled the bag tightly to his body and looked up at Diana Sanford. Only she wasn't looking at him but was frowning at the girls sauntering down the middle of the hall. "I didn't see you there."

Diana shook her head as she watched the girls go. "I wasn't saying 'excuse me' to you. I was talking to them." She turned to face him, and he watched her bright smile go tight at the corners. She clutched the backpack she had slung over her shoulder and took a small step back toward the lockers.

That step. He tried not to take it personally. Still, he couldn't help thinking about this summer at Sitto's when he walked with others without a single person stepping back from him. People smiled as they passed him on the street. No one thought twice about what he looked like or jumped to conclusions about what his appearance meant.

"Did you have a good summer?" he asked quietly.

"Sure." She nodded and shifted her weight. "It was good to have time away from school. How was your summer? Did you do something fun?"

"I visited family."

Her smile vanished. "Family is always interesting." She looked down at her own bag then off toward the media center. "Speaking of family, mine is going to be mad if I don't get my yearbook stuff done in time to get home and change. I should go."

"I need to get going too," he said as she hurried down the hallway. She glanced to the side once, and he saw her smile return. Not the tense one she'd worn for him, but one that seemed to be as bright as the sun. Diana stopped and waved to whomever she was smiling at, then disappeared inside the media center.

When she was gone, he turned and headed down the hallway with his head up, hoping to see a friend who would ask him if he'd read the latest Superman comic to chase away the voices of his cousins from this summer. When they'd asked him about how people treated him back home and whether he felt his friends really accepted him, he'd automatically said yes. But with each day that passed and the more questions that were asked and comments made, he realized how different he was from everyone at home. He remembered the little slights and the snide looks, as well as the insults some of the biggest jerks in the school spat at him. If he was honest with himself, it was his cousins as much as anyone or anything else that made him come here today. They made him realize he needed to make choices about who he wanted to be.

He walked by a bunch of girls holding tape and posters and standing around their lockers not far from the stairwell. They all stopped talking as he walked by. As he headed into the stairwell, he could almost hear his cousins' voices telling him how he could never really be an American as a Muslim. It was only when he was halfway to the second floor that he realized he had been holding his breath.

"Welcome back, Rashid," Mrs. Skatavaritis said as she came down the stairs. She stopped and smiled. A large floral purse dangled from her arm. She must be done with her back-to-school meetings and was heading out to enjoy the rest of the day, but she still took the time to stop and ask, "Did you have a good summer?"

"I did," he said. "How about you, Mrs. S.?"

"Well, it wasn't long enough. It's never long enough, right? But it was a nice break, and I'm ready to talk calculus. How about you?"

When he just nodded, she laughed. "Don't worry. It's going

to be a good year. I promise." With that, she continued on down the stairs.

Rashid watched her go, went up to the second floor, and then headed to the bathroom near the science classrooms, at other end of the school.

He spotted Mr. Rizzo in his biology room, but as Rashid had suspected, most of the math and science rooms were clean, perfectly organized, and completely empty at the moment.

He hoped the bathroom would be empty too.

It was.

Quickly, Rashid slipped off his shoes and socks and rolled up his pants in order to wash and get ready for prayers. When he finished, he picked up his bag and shoes and hurried to Mr. Lott's classroom down the hall. The adviser of the robotics team had always been cool about allowing Rashid to use his room when a class wasn't in session. Once in a while, one of the other boys from his mosque would join him, but mostly he prayed alone. He liked the guys who went to his mosque, but they were more interested in playing soccer than in building robots or in the new comics being released. And their parents let them do all their prayers at home after school was over. Maybe if he liked soccer more, he'd get along with them better. But as much as he tried to be a part of their group, he never could. They were all Muslim, and while that made them friendly to him, it wasn't enough to make them real friends no matter how much he wished it was.

During his fifteen minutes of prayers, he spotted Diana walking by, as well as two teachers clearly on their way out of the building. But none of them seemed to notice him, which made focusing easier than normal.

Rashid rolled down his pants, put his shoes back on, and picked up his bag. Then he went back to the bathroom. For several long moments, he studied his face in the mirror, trying to see what Diana saw today that had made her step back from him. What made so many of them do the same?

Dark skin. Curly hair. A long, scraggly beard. Just one more thing that made him different. This summer all the men in Palestine had beards, and his cousins, who didn't, were jealous of his because it made the older girls look twice at Rashid.

People stared at him here, too, but as his cousins pointed out, it wasn't because of his appearance. The more he thought about it, the more he realized that even after he had been living here for five years, most people couldn't get past what they saw on the outside. Fewer still wanted to learn. Not even his friends seemed comfortable enough to ask questions. His cousins said it was because people were scared of what they would learn if they asked. His father told him that time would bring understanding.

Rashid wished he could believe his father was right and that if he just waited long enough, people would act normal around him again. That they wouldn't look at him and see Muslim first and Rashid second.

The Koran, too, instructed him to wait in patience. It told

him to celebrate Allah while waiting and that patience is what brought strength and prosperity. But Rashid wasn't in the world that his father grew up in. The more he looked around, the more he saw the world as his cousins and some of the men at the mosque saw it. A world that looked at him with fear simply because he was alive.

Rashid had tried patience, but waiting wasn't going to fix his problems. If he wanted things to be different, he would have to try something else.

One by one, Rashid checked to make sure nobody was in the bathroom stalls. Then he carefully set his bag on one of the sinks and unzipped it. Ignoring the hammering of his heart and the shaking of his hands, he pulled out his tools and hoped his father would be able to understand that this was what Rashid had to do.

11:05 A.M.

CAS

— CHAPTER 8 —

PIECE BY PIECE, Cas assembled her clarinet. When the instrument was together, she took a seat on the piano bench and began to play.

Mozart. Her favorite.

Not for the first time, Cas wished she played the piece better. It was one she'd started learning before she'd had to leave her last school. She'd been determined to get it as perfect as she could. Only her schedule last year didn't give her as much time to practice as she needed. And at home . . . well, everyone else needed quiet when they were doing homework or when her mother was on the phone. When her father was around, he always said she should go for a run.

So to avoid conflicts at home, she'd practiced here fifteen minutes before and after school and eventually during her half-hour lunch period. Music was the one thing that made her happy. And when she played something beautiful, she almost could convince herself that she was beautiful too.

Sound filled the room. Cas closed her eyes so she could tune out everything else. So that nothing around her existed but the music and the need to create a resonant and pure sound.

The fingering still tripped her up. The tone got breathy, and here and there, she went off pitch. But it was better. And when she finished the piece, she started again to make it better still. Steady breathing. Leaning into each line. Feeling the flow of notes through her. Control of every moment. Maybe if she . . .

"Why aren't you in marching band?"

She jumped. The instrument honked. Embarrassment flooded her at the realization that someone had heard her make that sound and of how stupid she probably looked through the practice-room window while she played. Slowly, she turned toward the voice and almost fell off her seat.

Frankie Ochoa.

Football captain. Big man on campus. The guy everyone in the school recognized but she'd never talked to—not once. She doubted he had ever noticed her at school, but now he was standing in the doorway, staring at her.

"What do you want?" she asked, glancing down at the bag near her feet. She let out a sigh of relief. The bag was zipped shut.

"I was on my way to the gym and heard the music. I wanted to see who was making it." He leaned against the doorjamb and hooked his fingers through the belt loops on his shorts. "You sound good. Way better than anything they're playing out on the field right now."

She waited for him to follow up with a joke. But he just

looked at her as if he was curious why she wasn't saying a damn thing.

"Thanks," she finally said.

"You're Cas, right? I think we had advanced bio together last year."

"Yeah. We did," she said quietly. He was a year older than Cas, but she was a year ahead in science, so they'd been in the same class. He'd taken his frog off the tray and made it dance while Mr. Rizzo was passing out the rest of the specimens.

"I don't know about you, but I escaped having any classes in the dungeon room this year. I'm like a plant," he said with a smile. "I need sunlight."

Everyone called Mr. Rizzo's room the dungeon because it had only two skinny windows, which didn't let in any sunlight. Mr. Rizzo tried to keep things interesting, but there were at least one or two kids every semester who fell asleep in that room.

Frankie stared at her again — waiting for her to speak.

Cas's stomach twisted as she tried to come up with a funny or interesting response that wouldn't make her sound like an idiot.

Thankfully, Frankie filled the silence. "I meant what I said, you know. You're good. Is that why you decided not to be part of marching band? Too talented for the hacks?"

"What's with you and marching band?" she asked. "Do you have a thing for polyester uniforms?"

He laughed.

"Not especially," he admitted with an easy grin. "But there

is something funny about watching people try to look digni-
fied while wearing purple-and-gold polyester. It's just not possible. I go to a lot of football games and have become quite the
connoisseur of marching bands and their uniforms. Ours is
the worst of the lot. Thankfully, we're in the locker room when
they play at halftime, so we're spared what they're trying to pass
off as music. It's pretty clear no one in that band practices the
way you do. Talent means nothing unless you take the time to
hone it."

Before Cas could decide whether Frankie was serious about
the compliment he'd just paid her, he looked down at his watch
and pushed away from the doorjamb. "Speaking of locker
rooms, I have to head down to practice." Frankie took a step
back. His expression turned serious as he added, "You really are
good, you know. I'm glad I got to hear you play." With that, he
disappeared down the hall.

Cas stared at the closed door—heart pounding, palms
sweating. Finally, she lifted the clarinet to her mouth to once
again focus on the music, but instead she kept thinking about
the boy who had just been in the doorway.

Frankie was popular. Always had a girlfriend and a crowd
of people around him and could do no wrong—kind of like a
modern-day prince. Which was fitting, since he'd been on the
homecoming court last year—something several kids had said
was unfair, since everyone was certain he was the one behind
the chickens found in the cafeteria the week before. But no one
ever said anything too loudly, because everyone knew he needed

to be on the field if their team had a chance of going to state. She hadn't thought he'd known she existed.

The star of the football team knew her name. Cas wasn't sure how she felt about that, or if she wanted to feel anything. To keep herself from thinking too much, she took a deep breath and picked up playing where she had left off—before Frankie had interrupted.

Low notes as open and full as she could make them. High notes that floated on the air. All the while, she watched the window in the door of the practice room in case someone appeared —telling herself she didn't want to be interrupted, but deep down wishing that someone else would come. When she got to the end of the piece, she played it again. Waiting . . .

It was stupid. There was no reason to think someone else would stop by and care that she was in here. But Frankie's visit had made her think maybe, just maybe, there was hope.

Every time she'd believed that things would get better, she'd been proven wrong. She'd found reasons to hope and always ended up feeling worse when the disappointment crashed down on her. But maybe if there was one more sign that she should reconsider what she came here to do today, she would. She would walk away from her decision. She'd try to change things another way.

She played the piece again. Louder. The notes cracked under the pressure. Or maybe it was her soul that cracked each time the tone broke.

She played louder still, no longer caring what the music

sounded like. Only caring about the volume. She wanted someone else to hear. To know that she was in this room. To care that she was . . . that she just *was*.

After the fourth time through, Cas lowered the instrument onto her lap. No one had heard. There was no other sign.

Cas wiped the tears from her cheeks and sat there for several heartbeats as the hope she'd felt faded, leaving the familiar hollowness of disappointment behind. Carefully she took the clarinet apart, removed the reed from the mouthpiece, and put everything back in the blue-lined case. Cas unzipped the side pocket of her bag and pulled out the note she'd written dozens of times over the last few months before tearing each of those earlier versions into little shreds. She placed the envelope on top of the clarinet before closing the lid and running her hand over the outside of the sleek black case. The clarinet was one of the only things she truly loved. It was always there. It never judged.

Taking a deep breath, Cas picked up her bag with one hand and the clarinet case with the other, then headed out of the practice room.

The band room was empty. Open instrument cases sat on chairs and were strewn across the floor, along with dozens of backpacks. The music-office windows were dark. Everyone must still be at marching-band practice. Would Frankie laugh when he saw them stumbling around in the heat and think of her?

Probably not.

Frankie had asked if she thought she was too good to be a

part of marching band. He'd said those words without sarcasm or a snide tone, and she wished he'd been right.

She waited for several minutes, thinking that if the band finished practice and came back in—if someone said hello —she'd change her mind. Last year, when she'd first stepped into this room, she'd been certain her family was correct. That everything from before wouldn't matter. That things would be different here, because this place was different.

They'd lied.

Nothing was different. And at some point, it would get worse, just as it had before. She wanted to blame her mom for saying it would be okay if she dressed differently and her father for saying she just had to act as if she belonged and she would. They didn't understand, and they refused to listen when she tried to tell them. They didn't get that she didn't fit in.

She wasn't skinny like the popular girls. She used to always say the wrong thing, so now she just said nothing. Frizzy hair. Stupid laugh. Pimples on her forehead that no cream could make go away.

This summer she finally realized it wasn't the other kids that were the problem or her father or mother or her annoying shrink. There was only one constant in all of it.

Her.

11:19 A.M.

FRANKIE

– CHAPTER 9 –

FRANKIE WATCHED VINCE CARTER throw an unsteady spiral to a talented running back who didn't have a chance in hell of catching the crappy toss. Vince still had a hell of a lot to learn.

Of course, the trick there was that Vince had to be *willing* to learn. Frankie's father had suggested Frankie work with Vince, since their families went to the same church. Okay, it was less of a suggestion and more of an order, but Frankie had gone along with it because Vince did have talent, and Frankie liked the idea of training the guy who would eventually replace him once he graduated. It was just too bad Vince was a pain in the ass and believed that he was better than everyone else —including Frankie—and had no problems telling people so. The kid didn't think he had to put in the work to reap success. Not like that girl, Cassandra. Even if she had a stick up her butt about talking to him, Frankie admired her sitting alone in that claustrophobically small room, practicing her ass off to be better than everyone else at the one thing she was passionate about.

Vince didn't think he had to earn jack. He just wanted Frankie to get out of the way so he could have his position.

Yeah—not if Frankie had anything to say about it.

Frankie stepped away from the building and waved at Ian Morgan, then slipped back into the shadows as Ian grabbed a ball and trotted over to one of the receivers watching the first-string squad run plays. The second-string receiver ran down the sidelines as Ian cocked his arm back and let the football fly.

The spiral was tight. Just the way the two of them had practiced this summer. Frankie had been surprised the day the sophomore rang Frankie's doorbell to ask for help with his form. But Frankie had been impressed on that first practice session. Ian never once said the words "I can't," no matter how hard the challenge Frankie gave him.

That's what Frankie's father always told him that winners did. They kept their eye on the prize and did whatever it took to reach it.

Ian's throw was a perfect bull's-eye—hit the receiver chest-level.

And Coach Anderson noticed.

Frankie leaned back against the wall and watched as Coach blew his whistle and started screaming about teamwork and keeping focused on the drills. He shook his finger at Ian and stalked around in a way that was probably supposed to be menacing but, in Frankie's opinion, made the coach look as if he needed to pee.

Finally, Ian jogged back to the sidelines, his eyes firmly on the ground in front of him. The kid must have really gotten his ass well and thoroughly chewed. He'd have to get used to it, because winners never just got patted on the back. Once they cleared the bar set for them, the bar was always raised and people screamed until you got over that one too. Once you were a winner, you had to stay the winner they expected you to be.

Frankie waited for Coach to blow the whistle. When it came, he wasn't surprised to hear Coach yell for Vince to get some water and for Ian to run the next play.

Frankie watched Ian take the field. Ian struggled to get his helmet on. It wasn't easy to act cool when you knew every eye was on you . . . counting on you . . . waiting for you alone to give them something to cheer about. Frankie had had to learn to be calm under pressure—even when he felt like he was about to blow.

Ian called for the snap. Despite how nervous he was, their hours of practice this summer paid off. Ian backpedaled and waited before launching the ball downfield.

Touchdown city, baby.

With a smile, Frankie got up and walked back toward the locker room.

"Frankie."

Everything inside him tensed as he spotted Tad coming toward him. The eyes that Frankie had found mysterious and intriguing were narrowed as Tad zeroed in on him.

Frankie glanced behind him toward the JV practice. Coach was still barking out plays. Ian and the rest of the guys were sweating in the sun, but Vince seemed to be looking this way. Damn it.

"You're not supposed to be here, Tad," Frankie said. "Didn't you get the text telling you not to come to school?"

Tad stopped walking. He folded his arms over his deep blue T-shirt and studied Frankie. "As captain, you get to tell the team what to do to get ready for the game and you can push us on the field. But if you want to tell me how you think I should live my life, you'll have to do it yourself. Not through Jimmy."

"It's the same text everyone got," Frankie said, taking another look over his shoulder. "We shouldn't talk about this here."

Frankie started to move toward the door, but Tad stepped into his path. There was a reason the guy was one of the best receivers around. He was fast and could usually shake the guy defending him. Great on the field. Not so great when Frankie was the one trying to do the shaking.

"Then where?" Tad asked. "You've been avoiding me."

"I've been busy. And I'm sorry if you're upset, but I don't want to have this conversation here. If Coach sees—"

"I don't care what Coach sees. I—"

"You should." Frankie grabbed Tad's arm. "If you don't want Coach benching you, you should go to the lake with the others. You shouldn't be here."

"Because you're here?" Tad yanked his arm out of Frankie's grip. "And you don't want people to see us together."

"No." *Maybe. Hell.* "This isn't me talking as your friend. My dad says a good captain has to have his teammates' back. Well, this is me, your captain, watching your back. I'm paying a visit to the JV's locker room, and I don't want you here, or people will think you're involved." When Tad cocked his head to the side, Frankie added, "Meet the team at Jimmy's. Go to the lake and get the hell away from here before you ruin everything."

"How do I know these top-secret plans aren't just your way of getting rid of me?"

"You don't."

Tad smiled. "Fine. You want me to go hang out at the lake. Sure. I'll do that."

Frankie let out the breath he hadn't realized he was holding. "Good. Jimmy will—"

"I'll do it, but only if you meet me in Mr. Lott's room in ten minutes."

Tad wanted to meet him alone in a physics teacher's classroom? The school was mostly empty and the second floor would be even emptier, but hell, no. "I get that you're pissed at me, but you can't stay here. Look, I'll—"

"Ten minutes." Tad's deep brown eyes met Frankie's. "Don't ignore me this time."

With that, Tad turned and walked back into the building, leaving Frankie to stare after him for a second before finally following him inside. Frankie squinted when he stepped into the hallway. The lights were on, but after being in the sunlight, he found the hallway dim . . . and empty. Tad wasn't there, and he wasn't in the locker room, either, as Frankie discovered upon entering it. The locker room smelled of new white paint that couldn't completely mask the odor of sweat that was so much a part of this place. Frankie checked his phone, then grabbed the bag he'd stashed there when he'd first arrived. Less than ten minutes until Tad wanted him to be upstairs. Twenty minutes until the team left for the lake. He wanted Tad to be with them. The two of them might not be on the same page right now, but he didn't want Tad to get caught in what Frankie had planned.

He texted Jimmy to let him know Tad was running late.

WAIT FOR TAD AND WHOEVER ELSE IS RUNNING LATE. DON'T WAIT FOR ME. I GOT HUNG UP AND I'LL MEET YOU THERE.

Jimmy's response beeped a few seconds later as Frankie was headed up to the second floor.

TELL MINDY I SAY HEY. WE'LL GET THE PARTY GOING FOR YOU.

SURE THING, Frankie texted back.

He was glad that Jimmy thought he'd ferreted out the reason Frankie was late. By the time Frankie arrived at the lake, the rumor that he and Mindy had been hooking up would be spreading like a wildfire, because it was what people expected from Frankie. It's what he expected from himself.

Tad needed to back off. Frankie had to make his own choices, and he had decided he didn't want to go down Tad's path. He shouldn't have even set foot down it in the first place. It was a mistake that no one ever needed to know about. If they ever did . . . if his father and Coach ever found out . . .

Frankie shook his head and ignored the way everything inside him churned as he made his way down the hall that led to the main section of the school. Tad could hang out in Mr. Lott's room. Frankie had come to the school today with a mission, and he wasn't going to let Tad distract him from it.

The second-floor hall was empty. Most kids and teachers had gone home by now to enjoy one of the last days of summer.

Steering clear of Mr. Lott's room, Frankie hurried around the floor, getting things organized, then went back up the back staircase to the next level. Just two more things to do, and he was out of here. If Tad wanted to hang around—Frankie shook his head as he made his way to the front of the school. He'd warned him. If the guy didn't listen, it wasn't his fault. Right?

Crap. The place wasn't completely empty yet. Diana Sanford stepped out of the girls' bathroom, and Frankie ducked back around the corner as she turned his way. He hadn't seen her since the Fourth of July. The night he had stopped by her father's party and spotted her in the shadows with one of her father's younger, but still way older than her, staff members. And the way she was looking at the guy . . . Yeah, was it any wonder that he decided it was best to cut and run? She might be the kind of girl his family thought he should date, but Frankie had never really been interested. If he hadn't ditched that party, maybe things would be easier now. But there was no changing the past.

He peered around the corner in time to see Diana step into the yearbook office in the middle of the hallway. *Damn.* That meant Mrs. Kennedy was lurking somewhere nearby. The yearbook adviser had a thing about no one being allowed to work in the yearbook office if she wasn't in the building—something Frankie learned last year when he had dropped by after one of the yearbook meetings and tried to see if he could get some sparks going with Diana once all the other students on the staff had gone home.

Now he had a decision to make. Wait for them to leave, or just get on with it.

He heard two voices shouting in a classroom near the staircase—Great . . . more people were up here—as his phone buzzed.

Tad was threatening him. Either come now, or he'd be sorry.

No can do, Tad, he thought. *I told you that you should just leave.*

Frankie adjusted the bag on his arm and pushed all thoughts of Tad to the side. It was time to finish what he'd started.

11:43 A.M.

TAD

— CHAPTER 10 —

TAD REFUSED TO LOOK OUT the door to see if Frankie was coming. If Frankie had taught him anything, it was to feign confidence, even if you didn't feel it.

Fake it till you make it, baby.

Frankie was king at showing the world what it wanted to see. Tad had believed the all-American straight-boy persona. He would never have questioned it, had it not been for Frankie letting down his guard and allowing Tad to glimpse inside.

And then he shut him out.

Tad's phone chimed.

TAD, WHERE ARE YOU? JASMINE IS HURT BY
YOUR LACK OF RESPONSE, AND SO AM I.

Guilt kicked him in the gut. He'd forgotten to answer his mother's text about Jasmine wanting to go to a movie.

He shook off the guilt and shoved his phone back into his

pocket without answering. If Jasmine's feelings were hurt, it had nothing to do with him. He was gay. Saying those words out loud to his parents and his brother had been the hardest thing he'd ever had to do until today. Some guys he'd talked to said their families knew they were gay before they did. Tad's family certainly hadn't.

"But you play football," was his mother's first comment. Like that had anything to do with anything.

His brother might have known. There was resignation, not surprise, on his face as he said, "It's your life, and you have to be who you are." But Tad, as their mother started gushing about loving him no matter what and wanting him to give everyone time to adjust to it and to really be sure how he feels before saying anything to anyone about it, heard his brother quietly ask, "Do you really want to single yourself out even more?"

No. He didn't. But he didn't have a choice. Just as he didn't have a choice that their father was white and their mother was black and that because he was both, he often felt he wasn't allowed to be either one.

Too dark for anyone to ever consider him white, and how many times did he say something to his black friends, only to hear someone quip, "Yeah, but it's different for you."

Yeah, it was, but not like any of his friends meant. Nothing was made easier in his life because his dad wasn't black. It was just . . . different.

He was tired of feeling different, and he got that his mother was worried and probably was hoping that one day he'd look at Jasmine or some other girl and suddenly yell, *What the hell was I thinking?* But her pretending to accept his choices wasn't making this any easier. He was tired of pretending to be what everyone else needed him to be. He was tired of having everyone else's needs come before his.

He was done, and if someone else got hurt—too damn bad.

He spotted a guy walking past the door and stepped back so he wouldn't be seen. The last thing he wanted was someone besides Frankie coming in here.

Tad pulled his phone out of his pocket. Where the hell was Frankie? He was through with feeling as if he was never going to be good enough. He was going to make sure people finally noticed how he felt. Frankie, his mother, Sam, and everyone else—all of them were going to see that things didn't vanish just because you ignored them.

Although it looked as if Frankie hadn't gotten that message quite yet. It was long past the deadline Tad had given, and still Frankie hadn't shown up or sent a message.

Tad walked to one of the narrow windows and studied the parking lot below, looking for Frankie's white Mustang. It was parked in the teachers' lot closest to the school—exactly where no student was allowed to park.

Figures.

But that meant he was still here, and Tad wasn't about to let him get out of this. It was time for Frankie to face him.

Tad pulled out his phone. A message from Jimmy had arrived, telling him to hurry up. They were all waiting around for him—captain's orders.

Sorry, Jimmy. You're going to be waiting a long time, because today, Frankie isn't the one giving orders.

EITHER YOU TALK TO ME NOW OR I START SENDING MESSAGES ABOUT US TO EVERYONE ON THE TEAM, he typed to Frankie, then paused.

He could just turn his back on all of this and go back to pretending that everything was fine.

No change. No worries.

He could go home and wait until Frankie was ready to talk. Jasmine and all his mother's friends would be gone. His brother would be done playing his music, and everything could just be normal.

Only *normal* sucked, and he didn't think he could live like this—not anymore.

He was tired of who he was and what he wanted being pushed aside because it was too much trouble for other people to think about.

Tad swallowed hard and walked to the hallway. Frankie had blown him off again and expected him to take it and be grateful.

Put up or shut up. That's what Coach always said. *Put up or shut up.*

Screw that.

It was time to blow up the status quo, and to hell with what happened next. People were going to start realizing that he could no longer be ignored, and Frankie was going to get a front-row seat for the show. Whether he wanted to or not.

Tad looked back down at his phone and hit SEND.

11:47 A.M.

Z

— CHAPTER 11 —

Z STOPPED PACING and walked back to the window to look down at the ground three stories below.

Watching.

Waiting.

He'd come in through the field-house entrance. No teachers were around. He'd passed only a couple of freshman football players who acted like they were too cool to notice him stroll by.

God, he hated this building. He hated the way it smelled of fresh paint and Lysol. Like it was new.

Only nothing about this place was new. They could paint and clean all they wanted, but as long as it was standing, the same old crap would be underneath it all.

Maybe he was playing with fire, being here now—watching the kids who walked through the front door thinking that everything would be okay if they just tried their hardest. He shouldn't blame them for buying the idea that everyone would get a fair shake. But all they had to do was look around and they'd see what was really what. They'd get that there were no fair shakes. No second chances. You were judged as having potential or being worthless before you ever came through the front doors.

Blond Homecoming Queen who had come up the steps earlier with her pink shirt and her perfectly brushed hair didn't want to think about that. Because life was working just fine for her.

Z spotted Mr. Casey walking from the faculty parking lot toward the school, and he gripped the edge of the window frame. How many times had he replayed Mr. Casey's words in his head? Hundreds.

Lazy.

Disrespectful.

Worthless punk.

Had he cut classes?

Yes.

Had he blown off homework?

Who gave a damn about anything some guy wrote two hundred years ago? Why the hell did that matter?

Mr. Casey knew he didn't give a crap. But he called on him for every single question. What character did what? What place did they go to for something? What did some colored light symbolize?

Finally, "Think you're too good to do the assigned reading, Mr. Vega? Did you have something better to do?"

"Yeah," Z had said, clenching his fists under his desk as

everyone in the room had looked at their hands or out the window—anywhere but at him. He'd looked right at Mr. Casey. He wasn't going to let Mr. Casey get to him. "Something like that."

"Well, you can stay after the bell so you can explain why you're above doing the work that everyone else seems to find the time to do."

He hated everyone for jumping up and clearing out as fast as they could the minute the bell rang, and he hated Mr. Casey more for the way he'd looked at him—as if he was worthless—and for what he'd said and for the fact that he could say it and think he would never have to pay a price.

"I told you not to do this."

Z spun toward the door. Kaitlin stood in the entryway. Her straight brown hair framed the frown on her face. "What are you doing here?" he said.

She crossed her arms over her chest and stepped into the room. "I'm trying to keep you from doing anything stupid."

"You have to go home." He hurried across the room toward her. "Get out of here, Kaitlin."

"Not until you tell me what you're doing in Mr. Casey's room." She lifted her chin. The look she gave him was a lot like one that his mother used to give. "You didn't return my messages."

"Maybe because I wasn't interested in talking to you."

Hurt swam in Kaitlin's blue eyes. He hated it, but he wasn't going to back down. He couldn't.

Kaitlin bit her lip and straightened her shoulders. "Look. I know how hurt you are and how angry you felt when you got that letter—"

"Stop!" he yelled. "I just want you to stop. I didn't answer your message because I didn't want you telling me what to do and what not to do like I'm some kind of charity case not able to take care of my own life."

Her eyes swam with tears. "That's not what I was doing."

No. It wasn't. But that wasn't the point. "Then prove it." He reached out and dug his fingers into her arm, and he saw her fear. He hated it. He hated himself. But he had no choice if he wanted to keep Kaitlin clear of what was about to happen. "Get out of here, Kaitlin. Now."

He pulled her toward the door, but Kaitlin yanked her arm away and stumbled back.

"Are you deaf?" he yelled. "What do you think you're doing?"

She rubbed at her arm and lifted her chin to look him dead in the eyes with the stubbornness that she'd shown that first day he'd driven her home. "I'm not going anywhere."

11:51 A.M.

DIANA

— CHAPTER 12 —

"**I** SEE EVERYONE ELSE has already left." Mrs. Kennedy walked into the yearbook room and looked around. "I'm glad you moved the meeting up and that everyone got here on time. I have some gardening I want to get done."

Diana smiled at Mrs. Kennedy, pretending not to hear the impatience in her voice or notice the way she tapped her gold-sandaled foot. Mrs. Kennedy had been working in her classroom down the hall. Now that the yearbook committee heads were gone, it was clear Mrs. Kennedy wanted to leave.

Diana did too. She glanced at her watch. Time had gotten away from her, but she was still ahead of her schedule for the day. "I can finish the rest on Tuesday if you want." Diana started to rise, but Mrs. Kennedy waved her back into her seat with a laugh and a shake of her head.

"It's okay, Diana. I didn't mean to make you feel guilty. Finish whatever you need to. I love that you take your responsibilities so seriously. I guess I shouldn't be surprised, considering who your father is."

Trapped by the compliment, Diana settled back into her seat. "It'll only take me five minutes. I promise," Diana said. "And I'll make sure to let my father know that you're a fan."

Mrs. Kennedy tilted her head. "I'm a fan of hard work in all forms," she said. "But I have to admit that the senator's new education safety plan isn't something I'm all that fond of. It's McCarthyism all over again. I still can't believe these are the kinds of laws we're seeing proposed these days."

Diana forced a smile. "My father knows the bill isn't perfect, and I'm sure he'd love to hear your ideas. With so much going on in the world, he thinks something has to be done to stop the growth of violence."

"I'm all for the law and order he and the president talk about." Mrs. Kennedy sighed. "I just don't think authorizing schools to violate students' privacy is the way to do it. And when you ask students to police other students, you give them license to use learned biases against one another." She pursed her lips and shivered. Then she shook her head. "Let's just say I hope the bill gets voted down and leave it at that."

Diana nodded, even though she knew her father's career hung on getting the bill passed. He needed a win, as did the country.

Mrs. Kennedy cleared her throat to break the silence. "Since we both want to get out of here, how about I make the copies while you get the sign-up sheet ready? Divide and conquer."

"Sure thing." Diana handed Mrs. Kennedy the schedule with a practiced smile, then looked back at the computer screen as Mrs. Kennedy left for the copier. *Thank goodness.* Now Diana could finish in peace and quiet. She glanced at her watch again. Yes, it was way past time for her to leave.

She printed the sign-up sheet and picked up the backpack resting near her feet. She then turned off the computer and headed out in search of Mrs. Kennedy to tell her she was finished. Only Mrs. Kennedy was nowhere to be found.

This was just perfect. Diana should have insisted on printing the agendas. Then they would be done by now, and Diana would be on her way down to the media center. Once she made that stop, she'd be able to get out of this place.

She looked at the clock on her phone as she went back to the yearbook room, trying to decide what to do. She had to get going. Maybe she could leave a note . . .

"Here you go," Mrs. Kennedy said as she strode into the room with her purse slung over her arm. *At last.*

"Thanks." Diana took the copies and placed them on the back table in a neat stack under the sign that said TAKE ONE. "And with that, I'm done," she announced. "Sorry I kept you here so long."

"Don't worry about it," Mrs. Kennedy said with a smile. "Now we can both get on with our day. I don't know about you, but—"

The desks throughout the room suddenly rattled, and there was a deep rumbling somewhere. Mrs. Kennedy's eyes narrowed, then widened, and she bolted toward the door.

Diana's panic spiked as something, somewhere, exploded.

What was—? Diana grabbed the closest desk as everything in the room started to shake.

Fire alarms shrieked.

A ceiling tile crashed next to her as she rushed past the desks with her backpack clutched against her chest.

That's when everything came apart.

The door frame cracked.

Dust swirled.

The floor shuddered again.

Wood splinters and tiles rained down.

Diana coughed and put her hands over her head as she raced toward the door.

Books fell off shelves.

The computer she'd been working on crashed to the ground.

Metal and brick smashed together in one deafening roar. Something slammed against the back of her head, and Diana dropped to her knees. Desks slid toward her. She screamed for help as the floor shuddered yet again and tilted.

Everything creaked and groaned. Terror clawed at her throat, even as she fought for calm and crawled toward the exit. No one would be able to hear her screams; still she yelled as she fumbled to find the pocket where she'd put her phone. She had to have her phone.

A file cabinet crashed into the desks, sending them flying toward her. She pulled the bag close and screamed one more time. The floor tilted and every—

We all live in a house on fire, no fire department to call; no way out, just the upstairs window to look out of while the fire burns the house down with us trapped, locked in it.

— Tennessee Williams

12:03 P.M.

DIANA

— CHAPTER 13 —

WHY DID EVERYTHING HURT?

Smoke. She smelled smoke.

Diana struggled to lift her head and open her eyes. Small bursts of light danced in front of her. The lights faded, and all she could see were dark and hazy shadows.

Where was she?

Then she remembered the scraping of metal and falling bricks, and her heart slammed hard in her chest.

The explosion. She'd been in the yearbook office on the third floor. And then there was an explosion, and she was still in the school. *No.* This wasn't happening. She had to get out of here. She had to find her bag and get out of here now.

Diana pushed herself up, got a foot off the floor, and smacked into something hard and cold above her. *Oh, God.*

She raised herself up again and used her back to lift whatever it was with as much force as she could. *Move. Please, God.* Whatever it was above her had to move. Her heart pounded harder as she pushed against it over and over again. Only it wasn't budging. Why couldn't she push it out of the way?

Move! She shoved one more time, but it didn't give. Not at all. Not even an inch. She was trapped.

TAD

— CHAPTER 14 —

TAD DUCKED HIS HEAD back under the table that he'd dived under the minute the building had begun to shake and the sprinklers had started pouring water. The table had shuddered as pieces of ceiling crashed on top of it, but it was still standing. He was intact. Unlike parts of the room he could see that had been wrecked by the explosion.

An explosion. Something that should exist only in movies and on the news. And here he was in the middle of it. Frankie was probably in the building somewhere trying to get out, if he hadn't done so already. Or maybe he wasn't as lucky as Tad had been, and the ceiling or something else had fallen on top of him.

Tad closed his eyes and took a deep breath as his heart pounded hard and fast and loud and . . . *No panicking.* Panicking was how the people in the movies ended up getting themselves killed. He wasn't going to go down in this building while cowering under a science table. No way, no how. He just had to stop freaking out and figure out what to do next.

CAS

— CHAPTER 15 —

FIRE ALARM.

The sound pounded in her temples. *Bwoop. Bwoop.* Everything was ringing.

That was wrong.

Cas shouldn't be hearing anything anymore. This was all supposed to be over. But her shoulder and cheek hurt. Something hard was digging into her side. Something heavy was pushing down onto her back, and the fire alarm was screaming.

And she smelled smoke.

Cas opened her eyes and closed them again as she coughed.

Dust. There was lots of dust in her eyes and burning her throat. Fear punched through the confusion, making it harder to think. She couldn't think, because nothing made sense. Everything was wrong.

She closed her eyes, then snapped them open again.

The gun. Where was the gun?

12:06 P.M.

DIANA

– CHAPTER 16 –

DIANA LOWERED HERSELF back to the ground and took a deep breath to calm herself but coughed instead. Dust and smoke filled her mouth. She coughed harder as she rolled onto her right side so she could see if there was a way out in that direction.

Nothing. She was blocked by twisted metal. The left was almost as bad. Light shone through some of the debris, but none of the openings was big enough for her to shove herself through. If she tried moving anything, it would probably shift other wreckage. The metal thing wedged above her could come crashing down and . . .

No. She wasn't going to think about that. Thinking about that wasn't going to help her out of this. She felt around for the backpack she'd had with her. Nothing. It was gone.

She couldn't do anything about the bag. She had to focus and try to find a way out of here.

She couldn't go up. She couldn't roll to either side. That meant she had to move forward or back.

Coughing, she squinted into the dimness in front of her, then looked behind. It was brighter that way. Light was good, right? Light meant a way out.

Z

— CHAPTER 17 —

THE SOUND HIT HIM FIRST. The wailing, high-pitched beeping.

Z's heart raced.

His mouth went dry.

A denial sprang to his lips as he jerked his head up and opened his eyes.

Where was he?

He'd expected to see nurses rushing in to answer the alarm. But he wasn't in the hospital. His mother was gone. The siren wasn't for her.

Desks.

Dust.

He squinted and pushed himself up to his knees. A chunk of something fell off his back as he looked up into the bright blue sky. He was at the school, and he shouldn't be able to see the sky.

That's when he remembered.

"Kaitlin!" He scrambled to his feet and shoved aside a desk. Where was she? "Kaitlin?"

Maybe she ran out. Maybe . . .

He saw Kaitlin's hair first. Then he saw the massive gray-and-black steel air conditioner that had crashed through the roof and onto her.

12:08 P.M.

DIANA

— CHAPTER 18 —

THE SPACE WAS too tight for Diana to get on her hands and knees. The best she could do was raise herself up onto her elbows and wiggle backwards inch by annoyingly and terrifyingly small inch.

Something hard jabbed into her elbow. She yelped and forced herself to keep going, because staying here wasn't an option. Not unless she wanted to die.

"I'm not going to die," she said, coughing as she scooted backwards again. She bit back a whimper as something tore through her jeans and into her flesh. *Don't think about it. Just keep going and get out of this.*

Her head spun as she tried to decide how far she'd come. A foot. Maybe a bit more, and that had taken forever. Or maybe it just felt that way. Her heart raced as she gulped in air and coughed from the dust and smoke. She shouldn't have been here. She should have said *Screw it* when Mrs. Kennedy told her to finish up what she was doing.

Diana looked over her shoulder. The light was brighter. She was going to get out of here.

She moved faster, pushing with her arms and wiggling back with her hips. The ground beneath her slanted a bit. That made it easier. *Come on. A little farther.* The light was closer. Just a few more shifts, and she'd be free.

She shoved herself back again, and something cracked. Loud. The ground beneath her shuddered and tilted, and then she started to slide.

Metal groaned.

Tile and debris and shards of metal scraped her arms as she desperately reached for something to grab on to. Anything. There had to be something to grab. She wasn't going to—

Her hand cracked against something hard. Pain shot up her arm. She screamed. Then she couldn't breathe, because suddenly, there was nothing beneath her legs. She was going to fall. *Oh, God.*

"Help!" she yelled as her searching fingers wrapped around something cold and hard—a desk leg. She jolted to a stop and struggled to keep her hold. The weight of her legs pulled at her, threatening to make her lose her grip, which was slick with sweat and probably blood. This was bad.

"Help!"

Diana struggled to hold on while moving her other arm to grab hold as well. *Got it.* She felt a surge of triumph that faded as she tried to pull herself up and barely moved an inch. *Come on, Diana. You can do it.*

Metal groaned again.

The desk leg she was holding moved. Everything around her was moving, and now there was enough light that she could see the large metal filing cabinet looming above her head.

The desk leg trembled. She kept her grip, barely, as it jolted to a stop, but other desks around it were moving, and the cabinet above started to tilt.

"Help me!"

The cabinet was going to come down. She was going to be crushed.

Everything creaked and moaned and shuddered, and she did the only thing she could do to keep from dying as the metal cabinet started to fall. Diana closed her eyes, and, feeling the scream build in her throat, she let go.

TAD

– CHAPTER 19 –

"**HELLO?**" **TAD YELLED,** hoping there was someone around to hear him. "I'm stuck in here!" He listened hard for a response. Any response. The smell of smoke was growing stronger. *Holy hell.*

"Hello" he yelled again. "Anyone out there?"

No one yelled back. All he could hear was that idiotic fire alarm. As if everyone trapped in this hole didn't know they were in trouble.

"Hello!" Still no answer.

The fire alarm stopped screaming.

That should be a good sign, right? He tried to tell himself that someone who knew what they were doing had shut it off.

Only the quiet made it all worse. Now he could hear his breathing coming fast and shallow and the dripping of water from above. The water was no longer pouring out. Just drip, drip, dripping. The sound of each drop made him clench his teeth.

And the smell of smoke was getting stronger.

He listened harder for the sound of voices. Nothing. Just water and a creaking sound of something metal swaying somewhere. The same kind of creaking noise his swing set used to make.

Creak. Creak. Drip. Drip. Creak. Creak. Drip. Drip. This was all like something out of a slasher flick. And in those movies, the guy in the Goodwill dress shoes and screwed-up fancy tux always died.

"Be calm. Be cool," Tad said aloud, because it was better hearing his own voice than the dripping and creaking and the creepy silence. "Don't do anything stupid."

Something smashed on top of the table he was crouched beneath, and Tad scrambled out from under it. *Time to get out of here.*

Tad pushed himself to his feet and wiped his wet, dirty hands on his legs. The crisp crease of the rented tux pants seemed stranger than the broken room.

He looked toward the window. Maybe he could see if the Mustang was out there and if Frankie was trapped in this mess with him. If so . . .

The floor groaned. A section near the window cracked. Yeah —looking for the Mustang would have to wait. He had to get out of this room first.

He spun and looked around for the exit. There were broken tables and tiles and random stuff piled in front of the closed door.

Tad held his breath with the first few steps, waiting to fall through the floor at any minute. But it held. By the time he reached the area near the door and started climbing over the broken tables and chairs, he was feeling more confident. He was getting out of this mess.

Tad turned the door handle and pushed. The door opened three inches, then came to an abrupt stop.

Damn. Something must be blocking it.

Well, if football taught him anything, it was how to hit something hard. He set his feet, took a deep breath, rammed the door with his shoulder, and fell face first into the door frame when the door moved.

CAS

− CHAPTER 20 −

Ow. CAS CRACKED HER ANKLE on something buried in the rubble as she looked for whatever had made the sound she had just heard.

"Hello?" Was it just a falling piece of tile, or was someone there?

The school had been mostly empty when she had climbed the stairs to the third floor that morning. There had been three or four people on the second floor. A guy had been arguing with someone in a room near the stairs on this floor. Maybe it was one of them she was hearing.

She went still. There was the sound again. A chirping ring that was almost impossible to hear under the screaming of the fire alarm.

It was her phone.

She spotted her bag peeking out from under an overturned chair and scrambled to get to it.

She smacked her knee and bit back a yelp as she stumbled

over the debris and reached for her bag. *Got it.* She yanked it toward her and almost lost her balance again when it snagged on a bent desk leg.

Cas tugged the strap and pushed at the desk. It was stuck. *Really?* Cas pulled harder on the desk, lost her grip, and fell backwards.

She shrieked as she crashed into the broken tile and boards, pulling the desk she'd been trying to move with her.

Finally, everything stilled and her bag was free.

Gulping back tears, she picked up the bag and spotted the glint of metal beneath it. Heart racing, she squatted down and grabbed the gun. The one that had been in her hands when the world blacked out. Shoving it into her bag, she heard the chirping sound again. Cas dug into the side pocket and was relieved to find her phone. She hadn't lost it or the gun. And her mother was calling.

"Mom?" she yelled as the fire alarm continued to shriek.

"Cas? Where are you? Are you outside the school?"

"I'm in the art room." Or what was left of it. She looked at the desks and broken ceiling boards that she would have to move in order to get out.

"Where is the art room?" her mother asked. When Cas didn't answer right away, her mother shouted, "Cassandra? Are you there? Where is the art room?"

"The third floor."

"Oh, my God. Oh, Cas. There was a bomb. They said on

the news someone put bombs in the school and is setting them off."

A bomb. A bomb exploded.

"It's going to be all right, honey," her mother sobbed. "Honest. I'm coming. I'm coming and I'm going to get you out of there and it's going to be all right."

All right? This was about as far from all right as she could get. And it wasn't going to be all right. When was her mother going to understand that? Cas shoved a piece of tile out of her path to the door with her free hand but couldn't budge the next board. She needed both hands.

"Mom—"

"I'll call your father. He'll know what to do. Your father always knows what to do."

"Mom."

"The firefighters are on their way. The news said first responders are coming from all over. It sounds like there is some sort of issue about whether they can enter the building, but they train for this—"

"Mom—"

"Don't panic and be careful. You'll get out. Look for a door or a window or—"

"Mom!" she yelled. Finally her mother went silent. "Listen to me. I have to use both hands to move the stuff that's blocking the door so I can get out. So I have to hang up now."

"No. Cas. No. Just put the phone down so I can hear what's happening. Please. I have to hear that you're okay. You can't hang up on me, because I have to know. I don't think I could handle not knowing."

Horns honked on her mother's side of the call. Her mother yelled at some other driver to stay in their lane. *Oh, God.* Her mother was going to crash her car if she stayed on the line, and Cas was going to go nuts if she had to keep listening to her mother tell her it was going to be okay. It wasn't going to be okay!

Her mother's panic was making all of this worse. Cas looked down at the gun in her hand as her mother yammered about firefighters and police officers and some friend of Dad's who worked in the mayor's office. And Cas started to giggle through her tears. Nothing about this was funny, but it was. Because there was smoke and her ankle throbbed and she was trapped on the third floor of a bombed building and whatever phone call Dad made to the mayor's office wasn't going to help.

"Mom. I have to save my battery, and you have to drive home. Tell everyone . . ." she took a deep breath as the fire alarm suddenly stopped screaming. The smell of smoke was stronger. Sweat was dripping down her leg. So was blood. She pictured her little sister and the kitten she made Cas admire a dozen times, and the bubble of amusement popped. "Tell everyone I love them. Okay?"

Before her mother could respond, Cas hung up.

12:10 P.M.

TAD

– CHAPTER 21 –

TAD'S FOOT CONNECTED with something soft. He looked down, choked back a scream, and stumbled back against the lockers.

A person.

Holy hell.

He'd been slamming the door against a person. One who wasn't moving.

Bile burned the back of his throat. He gagged as he made himself kneel.

"Hey." He shook the guy's shoulder. When the man didn't move, Tad took a deep breath and rolled him over.

Eyes stared blankly. Blood coated the floor. Mr. Rizzo, the biology teacher. He had a piece of splintered wood sticking out of his stomach and blood leaking all over the place.

Nausea bubbled and pushed upward as Tad forced himself to take the teacher's pulse. Nothing. Tad's skin crawled, and he scrambled backwards. His stomach cramped. Tad doubled over and threw up. He shook as his stomach emptied and emptied again, until there was nothing more to come out.

Slowly, he pushed himself up to his feet, his legs shaking. Sweat dripped down his forehead. Goddamn, he wanted out of here. He started to take a step away, then looked back down at Mr. Rizzo. He knew he couldn't hear him, but still Tad said, "I'm sorry, man. Someone will come back and find you. I promise." For a second, Tad stared at the dead teacher he'd hit with the door. Then he turned to look down the hall.

Everything was trashed. The ceiling was collapsed in places to his right. There were art desks and paint cabinets and crap that must have fallen from the floor above that were blocking the staircase entrance to his left, and water was dripping everywhere. Lockers were opened and debris lined the hallway to the left, but from this end, it looked in better shape down there than here. *Time to move.*

Racing down the hall, Tad slipped on the wet tile and almost crashed to the floor. *Slow and steady wins the race,* he told himself as he spotted the entrance to the stairwell. It wasn't blocked.

Tad kicked something that went flying into the wall with an echoing crash as he ran toward the stairs. He had to get down to the first floor. The front atrium entrance was mostly glass and was probably completely demolished. But there were other exits and a ton of windows to escape from if he could just get down—

"Hello?"

Tad stopped and held his breath. There was dripping and the sound of something buzzing and —

"Is someone there? Can you please help me?"

He stilled at the sound of a voice. When the guy called out again, Tad let out the breath he had been holding. It wasn't Frankie.

Tad looked over his shoulder at the stairwell. If he got out of the school, he could tell the firefighters that there was someone trapped on this floor. They had the training to deal with this crap. He'd probably make things worse if he tried to move something he shouldn't and maybe bring the whole building down.

But if Frankie was still in here somewhere and heard someone yelling for help, he wouldn't run for the exit. Frankie would be the hero everyone assumed he was. He'd say it was his job as captain to tell Tad to beat a path to safety and let him handle saving the day.

Well, screw that.

Tad turned and headed back down the hall as fast as he could without looking at Mr. Rizzo's lifeless body. As he navigated the debris, he listened for the guy to yell again.

Come on, man. Give me another signal.

"Hey, is someone here?" Tad hollered as he got closer to the cave-in of desks and two-by-fours and tons of other junk that must have once been on the floor above this one. *This sucks.* "Hello! Anyone there?"

No response.

Come on. Yell again. "Hey. Is anyone there?"

"Hello?" the voice came again, and it sounded as if it was just on the other side of that mess.

Everything in Tad screamed to get out while he could.

He pictured Mr. Rizzo's lifeless eyes.

God, he hated this.

"Hang tight. I'm coming." Tad grabbed a two-by-four, yanked it out of the rubble, and threw it behind him. Then he tugged another free. All he needed was just enough space to tunnel through, find the guy, and bring him out.

Another board. Some tile. *Good enough.* He climbed over a desk and around a bunch of beams. "Hey, man, can you hear me? Tell me where you are."

"In the bathroom."

Which was currently blocked by a piece of the ceiling that had fallen in. *Awesome. Just freakin' awesome.*

Tad studied the wreckage, pulled hard at another board, and stumbled back as it came free. He threw it to the side, and as he reached for another, he was pitched forward as the school rocked with another explosion.

Dust and bits of tile fell from the ceiling. The boards and desks shook. Metal groaned somewhere behind him.

The stairs.

He looked through the dust and yelled "No!" just as the stairs he'd almost fled down and the area around it collapsed.

CAS

– CHAPTER 22 –

"HELLO? IS SOMEONE THERE?" a guy called from somewhere beyond the door. The shaking had stopped—again.

"Hello?" the voice shouted. This time louder. "Hey. Anyone there? Are you okay?"

"I'm in here." She spun toward the guy's voice and yelled back, "I'm in here and there's something blocking the door! I'm trying to move it and need some help!" She waited for him to respond. When he didn't, she shouted, "Hey! Are you still out there?"

"Yeah. Sorry. There are a bunch of things I have to get around to get to you. This might take a couple minutes. Hang tight and relax."

Not in this lifetime. The smell of smoke was getting stronger. She might have come to the school to die, but she hadn't wanted it to happen like this. That made no sense, even to her, but it's the way things were. At least for now.

Cas turned from the door and plowed through the rubble to

the only window she could see. The room used to have two, but the one near the front of the room was buried behind . . . God only knew what.

"You okay in there?" the guy yelled as something thudded on the other side of the door.

"I'm still here." Which was far from okay. "I'm going to the window. Maybe I can see what's happening." *Or find a way out.* When she'd picked this room today, she hadn't considered ever needing to leave it. For some reason, that struck her as horrifically amusing.

"Keep me posted. I'm Frankie Ochoa, by the way."

Cas froze. Sirens from outside grew louder. The firefighters had arrived. And so had Frankie.

She thought about earlier in the practice room. The way the words they exchanged almost made her change her mind. How if he had returned then, she might not be here now. "I'm Cassandra Armon."

"Cassandra," he called over something scraping, "it's nice to meet you." He grunted, and she heard something hit the floor on his side. "I should have that door open in no time. Just hang in there."

"Okay." Telling herself it was stupid to be disappointed that he didn't automatically recognize her full name, she pushed a chair out of the way and pulled herself up onto an overturned cabinet.

The smoke was getting thicker. She squinted toward the

front of the room. It was coming in through the vent near the ceiling, not far from where a clock used to be.

Waking up in what looked like a war zone was scary. The idea of being burned to a crisp was paralyzing.

As quickly as she could, Cas lowered herself down from the cabinet, limped around a broken desk, and got close enough to see out the window. The view looked nothing like it had when she'd stood here earlier, gathering her courage.

The sun was still shining through the cracked glass. The sky was still blue. But now, instead of seeing the white brick and windows across the way and to her left, there were gaping holes where classrooms should be. And a body . . . Oh, God, there was a crumpled body down below, sprawled on top of a picnic table. A woman? Cas thought so, but she couldn't see who, and whoever it was wasn't moving. Not at all.

Cas jerked her attention back up to the third floor and saw flames. Fire licked the bricks and roof above one of the windows of a room facing the back of the courtyard, scorching the walls black.

How long until it spread? She could see water gushing from the hole in the side of the building to her left, which would help keep the fire contained on that side, but if it came this way, where the sprinklers weren't working . . .

Cas climbed back toward the door. She couldn't count on Frankie to get her out of here. Counting on people just led to disappointment.

"Ow!" she yelped as she caught her foot on something buried under the rubble, and crashed into the broken tiles and tables in front of her. Pain punched through her arm. She sucked in her breath and went still, hoping it would stop.

Oh, God.

Agony flooded her. She shifted to take the pressure off her arm. Her vision swam. The world spun, and as it did, she saw blood. Lots of it, oozing from a jagged tear in her forearm. Somewhere in the distance, she heard Frankie yell over the pounding of her heart, "I can't open the door!"

She was going to get her wish, she thought as she grabbed for a splintered desk. She really was going to die.

12:14 P.M.

RASHID

— CHAPTER 23 —

RASHID PUT HIS HANDS on wet tile, pushed himself to his feet, and felt around for the hallway door that he'd let go of when the shaking had started for the second time, plunging the bathroom into blackness.

He gagged at the taste of blood and squinted into the blackness. His heart thundered in his ears, louder and louder blocking out everything else. There was only darkness and terror.

Wait. Where was his phone?

He'd had it before the second explosion. Where did it go?

Rashid felt around for it on the floor, trying not to get cut by broken glass. It had to be there. *Please let it be here.*

Rashid's hand closed over the phone, and he let out a sigh of relief when he hit the button and the screen glowed. The glass was cracked, but when he swiped the screen, it still worked.

Using the flashlight on the phone to cut through the darkness, Rashid found his bag under the counter, along with everything that had fallen out of it when it had dropped off the sink. He quickly grabbed everything, wiping off the Koran as best he could before shoving it all in his bag. Then, glass crunching beneath his shoes, Rashid crossed to the door and pulled it open.

There was a wall of debris blocking the opening. There was no way he could get out of this room on his own. He was stuck here. He might die here.

"Hello?" he yelled. "Are you still there?" *Are you still alive? Please still be alive.*

"Damn it!" the voice exploded. "We're trapped."

"Who's trapped?" Was there more than one person out in the hallway?

"We are!" the guy yelled. "The stairs just caved in, and now the two of us are both screwed."

"I'm sorry," Rashid said. "There will be another way out." There had to be. Rashid had to have faith. "Once I get out of this bathroom, the two of us will find it. And I can call for help. I have a phone."

"Did you call 911?"

"I made a call," he said, careful not to lie. His father always told him lies were a sin against oneself, and he was certain that dozens of people had already reported the explosions at the school. Help would be coming with or without his call. He looked at the debris blocking his exit.

"I'm going to try to push whatever this is out of the way!" the other guy shouted. "Move back. I don't want something to fall and hit you when I do this."

Rashid stepped back into the darkness and shifted his weight from side to side as he waited for something—anything

—to move so he could get out of here. Squatting, Rashid peered at a small gap that was letting in light and saw black shoes on the other side. Rashid heard a grunt as the guy tried to move things out of the doorway.

The guy swore. "This isn't working."

Rashid went cold. He was never getting out.

"It's all too heavy to move, but I might be able to shift this beam to the side and keep it there long enough for you to crawl through. Wanna try it?"

Of course he did. "Give me one second." He shoved his phone into the bag, then crouched down. "Okay. I am ready whenever you are." He hoped.

After a couple of seconds of watching the black shoes shuffle and get into position, he heard, "Get ready to move your ass."

Rashid held his breath and watched the opening. "Okay," he called. Each second felt like minutes as he waited for something to happen. Then, finally, there was a scraping sound as the thick beam blocking the opening moved a bit to the side. The gap was an inch bigger. Two. A couple more, and he might be able to fit.

"I'm not sure how long I'm going to be able to hold this."

Rashid could hear the strain in the other boy's voice and prayed his new friend could hang on just a little longer.

Another inch. The gap was almost big enough. Almost . . .

Now. Rashid gave the bag a shove and sent it through the opening, then launched himself through. All summer he had heard from his aunts and cousins and grandmother how he was too skinny. He was glad for that now.

"Move," the black-shoed guy said. "Not . . . much longer. Hurry."

He did. Rashid rolled onto his back and pulled his legs and feet through the opening just as the slab of debris slammed back down.

FRANKIE

— CHAPTER 24 —

"ARE YOU OKAY?" Frankie called.

"I'm bleeding."

"How bad?"

"If a vampire wandered by, I'd make his day. No effort required."

Frankie would have laughed at the joke had he not heard the pain and the tears. The girl still had a sense of humor, but if she was gushing blood, she wasn't going to be joking around for much longer.

He looked around for a board or something he could jam into the door to break it open. "Hang in there, Cassandra. I'm going to get to you." He never lost, and he wasn't going to start now. "While I'm doing this, you need to find a way to stop the bleeding."

"No kidding."

"Hang on," Frankie urged as he wedged a metal bar into the space between the frame and the door and pushed hard.

Something cracked.

"I think I'll sit, but thanks," she called back.

Funny. The girl was bleeding and stuck in hell, and still she managed to crack jokes.

"Elevate the injury if you can," he said to her as he wiped his hands on his pants to get a better grip on the bar. "They always tell us that in football practice. It slows down the flow of the blood, especially if you can raise it higher than your heart." Or something like that.

When she didn't reply, he yelled, "Cassandra?" Still nothing. His heart sank, and he pressed his ear to the door. He couldn't have lost her. He didn't lose. "Cassandra? Are you still there?"

He heard a muffled "Mhhhuh."

"What? Are you okay?"

"I'm trying to tie a bandage, and I only have one hand. So I can't talk right now."

He let out a sigh of relief and shook his head at his freaking out. "Sorry." Panicking wasn't going to help. Cassandra needed him to be the guy everyone saw on the field.

Come on, Frankie, he could almost hear his father say. *Time to show them what you're made of.*

Frankie positioned the bar a bit higher and pushed on it again.

Another explosion rocked the building.

Damn! The building around him groaned and began to shake again. Lockers flew open. Pieces of ceiling snapped and cracked and rained from above.

"Frankie!" Cas screamed.

"Take cover!" Frankie yelled as he got clocked on the fore-head by a metal bracket. He grabbed hold of an open locker to keep from falling on his ass. He thought he heard other voices calling out. Other shouts for help. Faint. But there.

More people must have been in the school than he'd thought —and one of them was Tad. Only he didn't have time to think about that now.

Coughing at the smoke that was getting thicker and warmer with every passing second, Frankie pulled on the metal bar, urging the door to break free. Wires above him hissed. Water dripped. Finally, something in the door snapped and gave way. He repositioned the bar again and pressed down with one hand while he tugged on the knob with the other.

Yes! He stumbled back as the door came unstuck and swung toward him.

"Come out, come out, wherever you are!" he shouted. Cassandra wasn't the only one who could make jokes in the middle of this hell.

And "hell" was the right way to describe the room she'd gotten trapped in. The back corner was gone. Where there should have been a wall, he saw hints of sky and lots of black, billowing smoke. The parts of the wall Frankie could see were buckled and streaked with soot. This part of the school was go-ing up in flames.

Where was Cassandra? They had to get out of here. "Where are you?" Could she have found another way out without telling him?

"What took you so long?"

At least that's what Frankie thought she said. It was hard to tell in the middle of the snapping, crackling, and popping from all sides. He turned toward the sound of Cassandra's voice, which was thankfully on the side of the room away from the fire and the missing wall and floor. The girl had been lucky, although he still couldn't see her.

"Sorry, I must have misplaced my key," he said as a hand came out of the rubble and grabbed the top of one of the art-table desks. Cassandra.

He leaped over an upended chair and raced around the wreckage as the top of her head appeared—dark hair that looked as if it had been sprayed by gray and white paint. And he recognized her. The clarinet girl from earlier today.

"Funny meeting you again."

"Or not so funny," she quipped back.

He flashed a smile as he knelt down next to her. Then the smiled faltered. Cas's olive skin looked like paste, and there was blood everywhere.

Her hands. All over her shirt. A streak on her forehead and neck. And dark stains were starting to bleed through the binding on her arm. She'd said the cut was bad, but the way she'd joked had made it seem less terrible than what he was looking at now. This was really, really bad.

"You okay?" he asked, even though he knew she needed a doctor and stitches and a real bandage, and she needed them as soon as possible.

"I've been better." She coughed. "I'll be great as soon as we get out of here."

"Sounds like a plan." He held out his hand to help her up. She wrapped her bloodstained fingers around his—they were cold. Everything around them was scorching hot, and her hands were cold.

He shook off the thought. "Okay, let's get you up and moving." *And we'd better do it fast.*

12:20 P.M.

RASHID

– CHAPTER 25 –

"**I THOUGHT YOU WERE NEVER** getting out of there!" Black Shoes shouted.

Rashid had too.

For a second, Rashid couldn't move. He couldn't breathe. He just stayed flat on his back, staring up at the wires dangling from the ceiling as his heart thudded.

Finally, he choked out, "Thank you."

"You're more than welcome, man." Black Shoes extended his hand to Rashid. "I'm Tad. Now, what do you say we get the hell out of here?"

Rashid stared at the guy's face, then looked down at the hand offered to him. Tad Hunter—who for some reason was wearing dress pants and a tux shirt—had just saved him. Football player. Track, too. And he hung with the guys who lived for hurling insults at Rashid whenever he was nearby.

Towel head.

Traitor.

Terr-ab.

Mosque man.

He waited for Tad to recognize him and for his hand to drop away. But Tad just stood there waiting. That's when Rashid remembered. His beard was gone, and without it, Tad didn't recognize him.

Slowly Rashid clasped the outstretched hand and let Tad pull him to his feet. Then he leaned down and picked his bag up off the floor, sending bits of dust and wood and tile flying. "Thank you," he said again. "I wouldn't have been able to get out of there without your help."

"Well, let's help each other get the rest of the way out," Tad said. "Dying at school isn't exactly my idea of a good time."

"I can agree with that." Rashid adjusted the bag on his shoulder and turned to look at what they were facing. There were cracks in the hallway walls, wet floors, and twisted lockers. Wisps of black smoke snaked around a pile of debris at the end of the hall.

The school was badly damaged but it was still standing. For now.

Rashid swallowed hard as he spotted a man lying near a partially opened door at the other end of the hallway. There was blood on the floor, and the man wasn't moving. "Look!" Rashid took a step toward him, and Tad put a hand on his arm and held him back.

"He's dead."

"He might just be unconscious," Rashid said, stepping toward the man. "We have to make sure."

"I did." Tad shook his head and turned so he wasn't looking in that direction. "I checked for a pulse just before I heard you yell. We can't help him. The only thing we can do is look for a way out of here and save ourselves. When we get out, we can let someone know he's up here. Okay? Where's your phone? We should call 911 again and tell them where we are in the building."

Rashid pulled his eyes away from the dead man and dug his phone out of his bag. Carefully, he swiped the cracked screen, dialed the number, then put the phone on speaker so Tad could hear.

"Due to the high volume of calls, our operators are busy and working to get to your call as quickly as possible. If this is not a true emergency, please dial 311."

"Are you kidding me?" Tad grabbed the phone.

Rashid backed away from him. "Everyone in the area must be calling 911." His father would be the minute he heard about the explosions.

Tad stared at the phone, then let out a loud breath and nodded. "Okay. Well, then I guess we have to find a way out of this mess ourselves." Tad stepped over a fallen beam and headed to the left. Rashid considered his options, then followed Tad as the message from the emergency line repeated, accompanied by the sound of running water and the buzz of broken electrical lines overhead.

After a minute of silence, the message played again.

"Maybe we should call someone else," Rashid said.

"Like who?" Tad kicked at a board and ran a hand over his buzzed hair.

"Actually," Rashid said, "I was thinking we could call some-one near a television." Tad looked at Rashid as if he had lost his mind, and Rashid quickly explained, "There will be television cameras outside. No one at my house will be watching televi-sion, but if we can call someone who *is* watching the news, they can tell us what parts of the school have been damaged and what looks to be the safest way out."

Tad flashed a grin. "That's smart. My mom was home when I left. I can call her." Tad's finger hovered over the screen.

"What's wrong?"

"I'm trying to remember the number."

Rashid stared at him. "You don't know your mother's phone number?"

"It's stored in my phone, so I don't normally have to think about it. Just give me a second." Tad took a deep breath, and Rashid clenched his fists and waited. Finally Tad nodded. "Okay, I think I remember it." He punched in a number, then hit the speaker button.

"Hello?" a woman demanded on the other end. "Who is this?"

"Mom?" Tad yelled.

"Tad? Oh, thank God."

"Mom, I need you to—"

"Sam." Tad's mother's voice was muffled. "Your brother's on the phone. He's fine. Just like I told you he would be." Her voice got louder as she asked, "Tad, where are you? Did you hear about the school?"

"Mom—"

"So far two bombs have gone off, and when you didn't answer your phone, Sam thought—"

Two bombs.

"Mom. Mom. Stop." In a slow, very clear voice, Tad said, "A friend and I are trapped on the second floor of the school."

Tad's mother gasped and made a choked noise.

Tad's jaw clenched. "We tried to call 911, but the line is busy, so I need you to look at the TV and tell me where the fire is or where the damage is the worst so we don't try to get out that way."

"Oh, my God. Oh, my God. Okay. Are you okay?"

"I'm okay, Mom. We're both okay." Tad looked up and shrugged. Which Rashid understood. No, they weren't really okay, but there was no point telling her that. Tad's mother started talking again, but Tad interrupted. "Mom, listen, we're fine, but we need you to tell us what's happening here so we can get out. Can you turn on the news and tell us what you see?"

"Okay. Okay. Just give me a minute to get to the television. Okay."

Rashid could almost imagine her bumping into things as she hurried to do as Tad asked. His family didn't have a television. His father said they were a distraction from the true purpose of life—although Rashid and his sister had noticed that whenever the Nationals were playing a big game, Father always wanted to take the family out to eat in a restaurant with a television. Without a television or radio, Rashid wondered if his family knew what was happening here at the school or if his message had been listened to.

"Mom?" Tad asked. "Are you there?"

Water dripped. Something creaked and groaned overhead. Rashid could hear Tad's mother breathing hard and saying "Oh, my God," over and over again. Suddenly, a loud but mostly garbled voice floated through the receiver.

"What's going on, Mom?" Tad asked.

"It's a commercial. I'll find another channel. Wait, here it is. They're talking to a teacher who was in the parking lot when the first bomb went off. Tad, they aren't showing the building. Why aren't they showing the building? There's a fire. They said before that there was a fire. They think a terrorist set off the bombs. You have to get out of there."

A terrorist.

"Just keep watching, Mom." Tad looked at Rashid, who nodded. "It'll be okay. Right now, we're okay and you're going to help keep us that way."

Tad kept talking to keep his mother focused. When Tad's

mother began to panic again, Rashid turned and studied the long hallway. It was in shambles, but he'd seen worse this summer on the sightseeing trips his cousins had taken him on. Gaza was filled with buildings that had been bombed.

"They're showing the school now!" Tad's mom shouted. "A lot of fire trucks are in the parking lot. And it looks like the fire is on the back side of the school, or maybe on the side? I can't tell. But I see smoke on the screen. Wait. The front entry doesn't look like it's on fire. Go out that way. Go now, Tad. You have to get out."

Fire on the back side of the school and maybe on the first floor in the hallway to their right. He and Tad were in the hallway nearest to the front of the school right now, but both sets of stairs leading down were blocked.

Tad ran a hand over his head and cut off his mother's panicked words. "We can't get out the front, Mom. If you can't tell where exactly the fire is, maybe we should just wait for the firefighters and—"

"No. Don't wait. There's something wrong. The reporters are saying that the police think the bomber is still inside the school. Oh, Lord. You have to get out of there."

"What?" Rashid turned and hurried back toward the phone.

"Mom?" Tad yelled. "Where is the worst damage? Can you see?"

"Oh, God. The woman is saying that the police got a message from the bomber. He says there are other bombs that are going to go off. If anyone tries to enter the school, he's going to set them off. You have to get out right now, Tad. The terrorist is still—"

Her voice disappeared. Tad looked at Rashid with wide eyes, then back down at the phone display. Tad yelled, "Mom?"

Still nothing. "The call must have been dropped."

"I'm calling her back," Tad said as he hit REDIAL. Nothing. Tad tried again and looked as if he was going to throw the phone when the call still didn't go through. "What the hell, man? No service."

Rashid grabbed the phone and looked at the cracked display.

No bars.

They hadn't changed locations, but something had changed.

Rashid hurried down the hall, looking for a zone where they could get a signal. But there wasn't one. The cell-phone signal in the school was never reliable. Everyone was always complaining about it, but he had a feeling this was due to something else. "The police must have jammed the cell-phone signal for the school. They must want to cut off any contact the bomber would have with the bombs or anyone outside who might be helping him."

"So they think the person behind the bombings has more bombs and is trapped in here with us?" Tad kicked a bent piece of metal, and it skittered down the hall and slammed into the door of an open locker. "What kind of terrorist takes out a school when school isn't even in session? It's not like we're some kind of major military target or a church or—" Tad went completely still. "Hold on a sec." His eyes narrowed as he turned his head and looked at Rashid. "I know who you are."

Rashid stepped back and balled his hands into fists at his side. Everything inside him tensed. Heat built inside him. He replayed all the insults in his mind as distrust twist Tad's face. Distrust that had become more and more a part of Rashid's life from people who thought they understood him. They thought they knew what he was. Was it any wonder he did what he did today? It was because of Tad. Because of Tad's friends and all the people like them.

Normally at school he turned away when the distrust surfaced. This time he lifted his head to look Tad straight in the eyes. Rage and humiliation burned hot as the floor shuddered beneath him. "No. You don't. You don't know me at all."

Not everything that is faced can be changed. But nothing can be changed until it is faced.

—James Baldwin

12:24 P.M.

TAD

– CHAPTER 26 –

THE BEARD WAS GONE. That's why Tad hadn't recognized Rashid. Without the beard, the guy actually looked normal. Kind of like he had when they were in English freshman year. Rashid hadn't had the beard then, but he had always been tall and skinny and quiet. Different. He looked the way Tad always felt — like someone on the outside, looking in. Tad used to think about trying to talk to Rashid, but that seemed like a good way to make people look sideways at him — something he had no interest in. He had just wanted to be as normal as possible in this place.

And that's when Tad realized something. "You never called 911."

Rashid stared at him with dark, unblinking eyes. "What?"

"When I called my mother back. There was only one 911 call on the list. You never called for help."

"I never said I did."

Of course you did, Tad thought. Rashid had shaved. He

must have done that to make sure people wouldn't recognize him, and now he was lying. Mom said the bomber had given a "message" to the cops. Rashid must have known the emergency line would be jammed and had reached them some other way. How else would Rashid have had an explanation handy for why cell-phone signals were blocked?

The smell of smoke was getting stronger. The fire had to be getting closer. He had to get out of the building. And the guy standing in front of him was looking seriously pissed, which made this even worse. Rashid had been timid in class, but this didn't seem to be the same guy.

"Look, man." Tad took a step back. "I don't care why you're doing what you're doing. I just want to get out of here before something else blows up."

Rashid stared at him then took a step forward. "You think *I'm* the one who did this? Why?"

Tad automatically stepped back. "How the hell should I know why crazy people do things like this?"

"Crazy people?" Rashid repeated. Anger simmered under the measured words. "What's that supposed to mean, Tad?"

Tad looked around, trying to decide which was the best way to run.

"You think I woke up today and decided to blow up the school because I'm a Muslim? Unbelievable." Rashid shook his head, turned on his heel, and walked several steps down the hall. Tad reached for a board sticking out of the pile of debris. He yanked it free as Rashid spun around and let out a bitter laugh. "And now you're going to beat me up? This keeps getting better. My family is Muslim, so to you, that makes me a crazy person. Well, maybe I should call the cops and tell them you're the one who robbed the house at the end of my street a few weeks back. After all, you're black. Aren't all black people gang members and criminals who belong in jail?"

"That's not the same thing," Tad shot back, even though it was. A splinter dug into his hand as he tightened his grip on the board.

"I'm sure you can figure it out. You've got everything else figured out, don't you, Tad? I'm a Muslim, so I must hate you. Fine. I *do* hate you, but it's because you're an idiot." Rashid jabbed his finger at Tad. "I didn't blow up this stupid school. I'm not a person who would do that, and you can believe me or not. I don't care." His shoulders slumped as he shook his head. "I just don't care."

"You're just walking away?" Tad shifted his feet and cocked the board back a bit in case Rashid was trying to get him to lower his guard. That's the kind of thing his brother would do to gain the upper hand.

Rashid lifted his eyes and met Tad's. "If you want to believe I'm a bad person, I can't stop you. But I for one do not wish to die in this building, and I especially do not want to spend my last minutes with you."

Tad stood tense—heart pounding and ready to fight. But Rashid didn't rush him or reach for his bag or anything threatening. He just looked at Tad with a sadness that made Tad think of the way his brother had looked at him last year when their dog had died. Then Rashid walked backwards and slowly eased down the hall, never turning his back on Tad. Twice Rashid glanced over his shoulder to make sure he wasn't going to run into something, but he didn't reach for his phone or do anything else threatening. He just moved farther and farther away.

Tad looked down at the board in his hand. His stomach turned. If Rashid had taken just one step toward him, Tad would have clocked him with the splintered wood. He would have beaten him until Rashid was no longer a threat. He'd never gotten into a fight at school or pummeled anyone. How many times had he walked away or ignored things the team was doing because he didn't want them to turn on him?

But he'd stood here, ready to fight Rashid. A guy who rarely spoke. When he did, it was never more than one sentence at a time in that quiet way he had. The dude never yelled or flipped out. Not even when Nicco and J.R. tripped him last year in the cafeteria or when the others called him names and bumped him into lockers as they passed in the halls. He just put his head down and kept walking. Rashid never showed that he was upset. He never struck back, even though he had to be pissed. Tad would have been.

So maybe the guy had a good reason to want to make people at this school pay. Maybe that's why he had blown the crap out of this place. To get even for all the names he was called and the slights he'd suffered. Maybe that's why he was acting so strange now and was lying about calling 911.

Or maybe—just maybe—he was trapped in this hell, scared and confused, just like Tad, and wasn't telling the truth because Tad had never given him a reason to trust him.

His chest tightened as Rashid continued down the long hallway. Rashid's words pricked at him like the splinters in the board he held in his hands. Because they felt like the truth. And if they were, what did that make Tad?

"Hey," Tad called as Rashid tried the handle of one of the classroom doors. Still holding the board, Tad stalked toward him. "I'm not a racist."

Rashid didn't look back at him and instead went to the next door and tried the handle.

"Hey!" Tad yelled as Rashid tugged on the door. "Did you hear me? I'm not a racist. Bombs have been set off, and you look different now and lied about calling 911. What do you expect me to think?"

"What I expect is for you to think and say exactly what you did," Rashid said, leaning against the door, which wouldn't budge. His bag slid off his shoulder and caught Tad's eye. The guy had brought that bag out of the bathroom with him. What was in the bag that was so important?

Tad didn't move as Rashid said, "I don't expect you to be any different from your friends."

The bag slipped lower on Rashid's arm, and Tad lunged forward. He grabbed the strap as Rashid yanked himself and the bag backwards. "What are you doing?"

"Who did you call?" Tad shouted as he pulled Rashid off

balance. "Show me!" he yelled. "If you don't have anything to hide, you shouldn't have any problem letting me see what's in your bag."

Tad tightened his grip on the black backpack. Rashid was pulling hard, but Tad had at least thirty pounds on Rashid and a lot of football training. This time when Tad tugged on the bag, he leaned his whole body back. The strap snapped. Tad stumbled back, tripped over a broken tile, and crashed into an open locker. Tad yelped and scrambled for the bag, which had landed not far from him. He reached for the zipper as Rashid charged forward and yelled, "Give it back!"

"No way in hell." He was going to prove Rashid was hiding something important. He was lying, and Tad was going to prove that he wasn't wrong for feeling threatened. He wasn't like the guys on the team who lashed out just because someone wasn't like them.

Tad juggled the bag and tugged the zipper down as Rashid grabbed the side and pulled. The backpack gaped open. Tad lost his grip, and everything inside fell out.

Tad dived to the side, covered his head, and held his breath in case anything in the bag exploded when it hit the ground.

Nothing happened.

No explosion. No fizzle. Nothing.

Tad opened his eyes. Rashid was staring down at the floor with an expression Tad couldn't read. Then slowly Rashid squatted down and reached for the bag that had fallen at his feet.

"Foolish," Rashid said in a flat voice. "It was foolish to come here today. I should have known better."

Tad looked at the items that had spilled out of the bag and to the ground.

A brush.

A bottle of hair gel.

Some notebooks.

Rashid grabbed a can of shaving cream and something else that had rolled under a piece of broken board and shoved both back into the bag, along with clothes and a bottle of water and a bunch of comic books.

Then Rashid reached for the phone.

"Let me have that," Tad demanded.

Rashid looked at the phone, then back to Tad. "Fine. You want it? Here."

The screen had been cracked before. This fall to the floor had shattered it.

"Who did you call?" Tad asked again.

"What does it matter?" Rashid replied. "You wouldn't believe me even if I told you."

Rashid picked up a T-shirt, and Tad spotted a book on the ground. Tad reached for it.

"Give me that," Rashid said, snatching the Koran from Tad's hands.

Tad let the book go. "You always carry that around?"

Rashid looked at him long. Hard. As if someone had hit the

PAUSE button on a video. Smoke was still snaking down the hall-way. Things snapped and popped and groaned around them. Tad flinched as, under it all, he could suddenly hear someone —a girl—scream. Rashid's eyes widened. He heard it too.

Still they stood there, looking at each other. Tad waiting for Rashid to explain the call or explain away the book. But Rashid just shook his head, shoved the book into the bag, and grabbed the rest of his stuff. "Someone might need our help," Rashid said, heading in the direction of the girl's voice. "Hello?" he called. "Where are you?"

No one called back. There was just the dripping and the sound of Rashid kicking bits of debris as he made his way down the hall.

Tad knew he should be trying to find a way out, but there was someone in trouble, so he followed Rashid. "Hey. If you aren't involved in any of this, why aren't you denying it?"

"Because someone needs my help, but even if there wasn't someone else here, there wouldn't be any point." Rashid stopped and called again. "Hello? Are you there?"

"You can't ignore me. I know what you're doing," Tad insisted. "If you were innocent, you'd be pissed as hell. You'd be taking a swing at me, instead of pretending I'm not here. You'd—"

Rashid spun, and Tad could see the guy was well and truly angry as he yelled, "You should know better! *You* of all people."

"*Me* of all people. What does that mean?"

"You know what it's like to be different, but instead of

thinking about that, you stand there while your friends hurl insults and believe everything they hear on television. You should know better, but you don't, so do you actually think my telling you that you're wrong would change any of that?"

When Tad didn't answer right away, Rashid nodded. "That's exactly what I thought." He turned again and jogged toward the other collapsed stairwell that Tad already knew was a no-go as far as an escape route. If the guy was really looking for a way out, he wasn't going to find one there. But if he was looking to set off a bomb he'd already planted . . .

You *of all people.*

Tad looked at Rashid, then back at the blocked stairs and the hallway near it, which was hazier than it had been before. That couldn't be a good sign. Rashid moved toward an unopened classroom and pressed his ear to the door. Then he tried the handle. When the door didn't open, Rashid went to the door next to it and listened.

"What are you doing?" Tad asked. He needed to be searching for an exit. Instead, he yelled, "I asked you a question! What are you—"

"Quiet." Rashid pressed his ear against the door and frowned.

"What's wrong with you?"

"Shut up." Rashid help up a hand and waited. "I thought I heard something."

Tad went still. "Something? What kind of something?" *Ticking? The cracking of fire?*

"I think the scream came from here." Rashid turned the handle. This door opened. Rashid pushed it open as far as it would go and peered inside. "Hello?" Rashid shoved harder, shifting a bunch of boards and debris that were in the way. "Hello? Is anyone in there?"

Leave, Tad told himself. But what if it was Frankie trapped in there?

"What do you see?" he asked.

"Hello?" Rashid asked again as he shoved the door all the way open. "Is anyone there?"

DIANA

— CHAPTER 27 —

DIANA KNELT UNDER the tall chemistry tables and tried to get her bearings. *Fear.* She could still taste it. Still feel it pulsing inside her.

Don't panic. As long as she didn't panic, everything would turn out okay. Her father always said that true leaders kept their cool in situations in which everyone else would lose their heads. She and Tim had talked about that a lot during the last few months. Success required the ability to do what had to be done without letting anything—like fear—get in the way. Her father and Tim never panicked. She wouldn't do it now.

She took out her phone and dialed Tim, while everything around her creaked and wires hung from the ceiling like a scene out of a bad movie.

No answer.

She frowned and crawled out from under the table with her cell phone in hand, then surveyed everything around her. Where was the backpack? She'd had it when she'd been dangling from the desk leg, hanging on for dear life. Then she'd let go, with nothing beneath her, and had hit the floor below feet first, sending a jolt of pain up her legs and spine. More pain when she'd crashed forward to her knees, almost smashing her face into one of the desks.

She had to find that bag.

She had to get out of this room.

Her thoughts tumbled over one another. She couldn't see the doorway to the hall. But there was another door on the side of the room that led to a pass-through closet, which opened to the hallway. The chemistry teachers used it for storage and as a break room, equipped with a coffeepot, a microwave, and enough microwave popcorn to feed the entire school.

Diana glanced at her phone, then back at the door. Could she get to the closet? If she did reach it, would she be able to get the door open? Maybe she'd find the bag on the way. If so, she'd—

"Hello?" a voice called.

Diana looked up, trying to decide where the sound was coming from. Must be from the part of the third floor that hadn't relocated to this level.

"Help!" The voice was closer. And it belonged to a boy. "Hello? Please? Is there anyone there?"

Diana checked the time, then slid the phone back in her pocket as the voice yelled again from above. "We need help!"

She looked around and spotted a couple of desks that looked like they were wedged firmly in place enough to climb.

"Hey!" she yelled as she squeezed sideways though a narrow

gap in the broken chemistry tables and reached the desks. "Hello? Are you there? I'm on the second floor. Are you guys okay?"

"Do you think anyone in this place is okay?" the boy yelled. The voice was vaguely familiar. "Kaitlin is trapped and hurt, and I can't get her out on my own. She needs help."

Diana could use that too.

No, she told herself. She wasn't the one who needed help, because she was the one in control. But if she wanted to help someone else, she needed to get back up to the third floor. Diana studied the pile of desks, looking for something stable to climb.

She reached up for a board and tugged on it to make sure it would hold her weight. Then she put a foot on a chunk of ceiling and began to climb. "I'm coming."

She had to try several times before she found a secure place to put her foot, then pulled herself up.

Ouch. A splinter dug deep into her finger, and she gulped back tears. Compared to the cuts and scrapes on the rest of her, it wasn't a big deal. She grabbed the beam tight and kept climbing, looking for the next desk leg or metal beam or cabinet that didn't shift when she took hold.

Looking up, she saw patches of blue. The sky and the sunshine and the bird that flew by seemed unreal. She could also hear the boy's voice from above floating down. It sounded fainter than before. He must have moved down the hall— *Great. Thanks for the support and help.*

Diana started climbing again, this time faster as she focused on the sound of the sirens that grew louder the higher she climbed through the gaping hole in the ceiling. More first responders must be coming—probably from other towns.

Diana shoved aside a chunk of ceiling tile and sent it thudding below. She was almost to the top of the chemistry room's ceiling when she spotted her red backpack in the wreckage beneath her.

"Hey!"

She jolted at the loud voice and pitched forward. She grabbed tightly on to a metal bar and yelped as it cut into the palm of her hand.

"You okay?"

"Not really." She automatically checked the angry words she wanted to hurl at him. Not ladylike. Not acceptable. Still they churned and pounded inside her head, fighting to break free. She closed her eyes and took a deep breath—two—three, then said, "But I'll live, as long as you don't scare the hell out of me again."

"Sorry," he said. "I thought you could see me, since I can see you."

He could?

Diana glanced around as much as she dared. She was high enough to see the third floor, or the part of it that hadn't collapsed to the classroom below. But what caught her attention was the smoke beyond the windows and the licks of fire.

She yanked her eyes away from the flames and craned her

neck to look behind her at where the exit had to be. A shadow shifted beyond the doorway.

"Do you need help?" he yelled.

"Give me a minute." She looked down one more time, then stepped onto a metal beam that at one point must have been a part of the second-floor ceiling, gasping when it shimmied under her feet. Her stomach dropped, but the beam held. Most of the floor between here and the door was cracked or had crashed down into the classroom below.

"I can see the doorway," she called. "But most of the floor is missing. I am going to try to walk along this beam, only it doesn't go all the way to the door. I might need a little help when I get closer."

Diana inched forward on the beam, using another piece of metal dangling from the ceiling to help her keep her balance. She held her breath and judged the distance between the doorway and where she stood. More than two feet. Probably less than three.

If she could get a running jump, she'd be able to get a whole lot farther than that. But on this beam, she doubted she could get much power behind a leap. If she didn't make it or the floor didn't hold, she would be in trouble. But as her father said, sometimes you had to take a calculated risk in order to earn the payoff. And she was going to need someone to grab her in case she totally screwed this up.

"Are you ready?"

Diana saw long, dark hair appear in the doorway. The guy stumbled and grabbed the door frame tightly as the floor beneath his feet began to give way. He jumped back just before a small chunk fell below, leaving Diana with several additional inches to jump. But now she could see the guy's face.

Z.

She stared at him, trying to decide why he was here. In school. Today.

She'd never talked to him, but she knew the kind of trouble people said he was always getting into. He was the last person who should have been in this building the week before the semester started, and certainly not the person she wanted to count on for help. All the piercings and tattoos didn't exactly inspire confidence.

"I need you to catch me on the other side, since the floor is falling apart." As he had just demonstrated. *Oh, God.*

Z looked down the hallway, then back at Diana. "Just tell me what you need me to do."

"Stand back one step," she directed. "I'm going to jump as far as I can. If the floor gives way beneath me, I'm going to need to grab on to you, and you can't let go." *Please don't let go.* "Got it?"

"Yeah, I got it," Z said as he took a step back and transferred his weight to the front of his feet like athletes did when they needed to be ready to move fast. *Good.* If his reflexes were faster than his intellect, she might have a chance. He glanced down the hall, then back at Diana. "I'm ready when you are."

"Great. Give me a second." She could do this. She wasn't the type to fail. It wasn't allowed.

Taking a deep breath, she slowly inched back so she would have a little room to get some momentum before jumping. Then, before she could think too hard about how stupid this was or why she was doing it at all, she looked down at the beam to make sure she was putting her feet in the right place, then hurled herself forward.

She locked eyes with the angry but solid-looking Z. Everything inside her tensed as she flew over the space between the beam and the doorway. She let out a whoosh of air as her right foot hit the floor on the other side just as her left shoulder collided with the door frame.

"No. Oh, God." Diana stumbled. The floor cracked beneath her feet. Frantic, she reached out for the door frame and screamed as she pitched backwards. A hand clamped around her wrist like a vise and yanked her through the doorway with such force that she lost her balance. She collided with Z, sending them both tumbling to the ground. Z on the floor. Diana sprawled on top of him — all the air knocked out of her.

Diana wheezed in a painful breath, trying not to panic at how hard it was to fill her lungs.

"Can you get off of me?" he groaned. "You're heavy."

Heavy? She'd just risked her life because the idiot asked her to, and he was calling her heavy? Seriously?

Taking in a slightly less strained breath, Diana put her hands on Z's black T-shirt. He grunted as she pushed hard against him and climbed to her feet. While he struggled to get upright, Diana checked the urge to kick him and instead felt her side pocket for her phone. There was no service. She had no way to reach beyond the walls for advice on what to do next.

"What are you doing?" Z asked, leaning over to look at the display.

She shut the screen down and said, "I want to call for help, but there's no signal."

"There might be one down here. Come on." He grabbed her arm and yanked her down the hall, almost pulling her off her feet.

12:30 P.M.

Z

— CHAPTER 28 —

COME ON. COME ON.

Z ducked low to get under a fallen beam and hurried down the hall, glancing over his shoulder to make sure the homecoming queen was following. Of all the people he could have found, it just figured it was her. People like Homecoming Girl, who thought they were better than he was, were the reason he had come to school today.

"Kaitlin, I found help!" he called, hurrying toward the caved-in section of the room where she'd been standing when the first bomb went off. Now her legs were pinned under a gray-and-black steel air-conditioning unit that had fallen through the ceiling.

Because of him.

He shook off the churning panic as he knelt down next to Kaitlin and took her hand in his. It was small. Cold. Weak. So like his mother's.

"Kaitlin, I brought help. We're going to get you free and out of this place. Right?"

"I told you to leave" Kaitlin said tightly. "You have to get out."

"You told me to find help." Z looked back at Diana with a look that he hoped would make her understand that she might think it was okay to kick him around, but she couldn't do that to Kaitlin. She needed help.

Homecoming Princess stepped forward. The floor creaked beneath her feet, and she came to a dead stop.

"The floor held my weight. You'll be fine." If not, he didn't care. The only person who mattered was Kaitlin.

To prove his point, he stood up and walked toward the side of the air conditioner that had smashed onto a desk. The broken wood beneath held that side a foot or two off the ground. The floor around it was cracked—but it still held his weight. "See. It's fine. I'm going to wedge a board under here and lift the air conditioner enough for you to pull Kaitlin out."

Homecoming Girl didn't move.

"Don't be stupid, Z," Kaitlin said quietly. "It's not going to work. You need to get out of here."

Her eyes were glassy. The freckles on her face looked darker than ever against her pale skin. For someone so small, she had a huge voice and a stubborn streak a mile wide. She believed anything was possible. For her to say this wasn't . . .

He wasn't going to accept that.

"We can do this, Kaitlin," he said, yanking a two-by-four out of a pile of debris. "Right?"

He looked over at Miss Princess, waiting for her to agree.

But she was just standing there staring at Kaitlin. Her eyes wide. Her mouth slightly open.

"Right?" he asked again.

Slowly, the blonde shook her head and took a step back. "No. Listen to Kaitlin. You can't move her."

"We have to," he insisted. She had to be okay. She just had to be.

"I get that you want to, but if we move her right now, she'll die."

The words slapped his heart.

"Look," the girl said. "At best, her bones are simply broken, but if it's more than that . . ." She took a deep breath and once again glanced down at Kaitlin before quickly looking away. "If she has other injuries, she could lose a lot of blood the minute we move her. We don't have anything to stop the bleeding. This is bad, but that would be far worse. And she's probably in shock." There had to be other options other than having her legs crushed or bleeding out. There had to.

"Z," Kaitlin whispered.

He squelched the panic and forced himself to give an encouraging smile as he walked back and knelt at her side. "I'm here. And I'm going to get you out of this. You're going to be okay."

How many times had he told his mother it would all be okay?

"I know you want to help, Z." Kaitlin closed her eyes tight. Her voice sounded thin. The pain was wearing her down. "But you have to listen to her."

Kaitlin's face looked even paler. Ghostlike.

"I'm not going to give up," he said. "You can't either. You have to keep fighting."

"Z . . ."

"Promise me you'll keep fighting, and so will I."

He smoothed her hair, stood up, and stalked over the cracked floor toward the shattered windows, wanting to smash something. To smash it all. But that would scare Kaitlin. He had to—

"Z?" Homecoming Chick's voice made him jump. He hadn't heard her sneak up behind him. "I'm sorry about your friend."

People liked saying that crap. As if they really thought someone would believe them.

"My name's Diana, by the way. Diana Sanford."

Of course it was. He should have known that's who she was. Senator Sanford's sainted daughter. No wonder she thought she was the authority on all things. "I'm getting Kaitlin out of here."

"Kaitlin needs paramedics or the fire department or people more skilled than we are if she's going to get through this."

"Well, where the hell are they?" he yelled while Diana looked down at the phone in her hand as if it were magically going to give her the answer. "I don't know about you, but I'm not seeing any firefighters bursting through the doors." He grabbed an overturned chair by the legs and swung it toward the window.

The chair and the glass shattered. Z leaned his head out and yelled, "Hey! We're up here. There's a girl who needs help right now!"

Dozens of emergency vehicles were in the parking lots, as were people in uniform. They were all looking in the direction of the school.

No one was rushing toward the building. A couple of fire-fighters took a step or two toward the edge of the asphalt, but no one came any farther.

"Hello?" he screamed. "What the hell are you waiting for? You need to move! A girl is going to die!"

"Z, you're not helping," Diana said as he pulled his head back into the room.

"Like you are?"

"I'm trying to. There's a reason no one is coming in."

"Like what?" he yelled.

"Like they think there's another bomb!"

Kaitlin moaned, and Z's heart tightened.

Quietly, Diana said, "Fire responders must have been ordered to stay out of the building until the bomb squad or robots or whatever determine if there's another bomb. If there is, they won't come in. They can't; otherwise they'll put us in even greater danger than we are now."

Which meant they were on their own.

If that's the way they wanted it—fine. *Screw them. Screw them all.*

FRANKIE

– CHAPTER 29 –

"**HERE'S THE PLAN.** We're going to get out of this room. Then we'll look at those bandages, and after we make sure you've staved off the vampires, we'll get out of Dodge. Deal?" Frankie asked.

"I think we have more to worry about when it comes to the smoke, but if you want to focus on vampires, sure thing," Cas said. She took a deep breath, then nodded. "I'm ready when you are."

Still holding her hand, he got to his feet and said, "Okay. One. Two. Three."

He pulled. She stumbled, and he snaked an arm around her back to make sure she didn't go down for the count. The back of her shirt was wet with sweat.

He adjusted his grip and guided her until she was standing all the way upright in the middle of the chaos around them. She leaned forward, and he lunged to grab her because he thought she was going to hit the deck again. Then he realized she was reaching for a blue bag that was on the ground.

"Let me get that," he said, picking it up before she had the chance. "I can carry it for you."

"I'll carry it," Cas snapped as she grabbed the bag and tugged. She almost stumbled as he let go. For a flash of a second, Frankie wondered what was in it and why Cas didn't want him to carry it. Then Cas started coughing from the smoke, and he went back to the most important thing on the agenda.

Run.

"Let's go."

He put his left hand behind her back to help guide her out of the room. She flinched when he touched her and tried to pull away, but Frankie held tight. The far wall looked almost ghostly through the haze of smoke. The heat was stronger still. And in the missing corner of the room, there were licks of red amid the swirling puffs of gray and black.

He and Cas stumbled around the broken desks and shelves and other crap. The girl choked back whimpers of pain, but she never complained. Although she probably wanted to when they reached the doorway and he all but shoved her through.

Frankie slammed the door of the art-room-from-hell shut behind them. The hall that led to the front of the school had collapsed. The hall going to the back of the school where he had originally come from had gotten hit in the second explosion—not to mention it was the same direction the smoke was coming from. It looked like the path was clearer that way, but . . .

"This way," Cas said, pushing away from the lockers with

her good arm and taking a step in the direction that led to the front of the school and the biggest of their roadblocks. "The art office has a door—"

"That leads to the storage room," he finished the sentence for her, understanding exactly what she was going for. "If we're lucky, we'll be able to go around the cave-in through the office and the storage room and come back into the hallway on the other side."

"How do you know about the storage room and the art office?"

"I take it you don't think a football player can like art?" he asked, shoving a piece of metal to the side before turning back to see if Cas needed help.

She was holding her bag tight against her with her good arm and looking down at the ground, ignoring his hand as he reached out to help steady her.

"Remember last year's homecoming?" he asked, putting his hand under her arm as she slipped and almost crashed into a locker.

"I'm not really into homecoming," she said, tensing under his touch.

Of course she wasn't, he thought, making sure she stayed steady as their feet crunched the debris. "Well, you might remember last year coming to school and finding all the homecoming posters had been replaced by ones that didn't take themselves quite so seriously."

They were also not all that attractive, since the four linemen he'd roped into helping with the project had painted about as well as a couple of monkeys. But he thought the posters he'd created with the paints he'd swiped out of the art department storage room urging people to vote for NONE OF THE ABOVE for Homecoming King and Queen showed a certain level of talent.

"You painted those?"

"And you thought I didn't know anything about art," he said, trying the doorknob. *Ha!* The art office door wasn't locked. *Bonus.*

He made a beeline for the storage room to the left. The door was locked, but the metal bar and a lot of grunting fixed that problem.

Inside, the small room was dark as a tomb. He stubbed his toe and swore as he held his hands in front of him, trying to find the other door. Then it took a dozen tries to snap that lock, which he blamed solely on the lack of light and not on his limited breaking-and-entering skills. Once the lock gave way, he said, "If you believe in praying, Cas, this might be the time to send one up." Then he gave the door a shove. It started to open, then stopped.

Damn it.

"We're stuck?" she asked.

Frankie shook his head. "Not yet. Give me some room." He took three steps back, squared himself like he would do in a drill, and bolted forward, angling his shoulder toward the door.

Oof. That was going to leave a mark.

His shoulder sang, and he bit back a yelp as the door flew open. He sailed through, stumbled, and went crashing to the ground on top of a bunch of broken boards and beams and water. *Ow.*

"You did it. That was amazing!" Cas yelled before asking, "Are you okay?"

"Too much power," he said, pushing off the wet ground, refusing to admit that it hurt like hell. "I'm fine."

"You're bleeding."

He looked down to where she pointed. A streak of red trickled down his calf from his knee. "Not enough blood for the vampires to notice," he assured her. But the way Cas was swaying and holding on to the wall for dear life made him pretty sure she couldn't say the same. How the girl was still upright and not complaining was beyond him. He wished the guys on his team had half as much grit.

"Take a seat for a second and let me rewrap your arm." When she shook her head and started to say they should just keep going, he said, "Please, Cas. Let me help."

She stared at him, then slowly sank into a chair. With both doors open, he had enough light to work with.

"Sparkly," he said as he slowly unwrapped the slick fabric she was using as a bandage.

"Yeah. And?"

"And you don't strike me as the sparkly-clothes type. No offense." He finished removing the bandage and was glad the light was dim. He'd been prepared for bad, but the gaping, jagged cut in her arm was worse than he'd imagined.

"No offense taken." She gasped as she glanced at the cut, then turned her head, pain flickering across her face. "My mother thinks girls are supposed to like shiny clothes. Crazy, right?"

"My dad believes all boys want to play football—I guess everyone has their thing. Hold still. I have an idea." He pulled his shirt over his head, folded it quickly, and pressed it firmly over the injury. Then he took the scarf she'd used before and quickly wrapped it as secure as he could around the T-shirt and her arm. She flinched, bit her lip, and closed her eyes so tightly that he thought her forehead was going to pop, but she barely made a sound as he pulled the fabric tight.

Most of the guys on the team would have had a hard time sucking it up the way she had. Even Tad would have had trouble.

Frankie ignored the way thinking of Tad made his stomach lurch, and he finished tying the final knot. Either Tad was still alive or he wasn't. Frankie had no way of knowing.

"That should do it." He wiped his blood-streaked hands on his shorts and looked back at the empty art office. Not much smoke. No fire . . . yet. Holding out his hand to help her up, he said, "Let's get the hell out of this place. What do you think?"

"Do you honestly expect me to say no?" she asked.

With more energy than she probably felt, Cas pushed up from the ground with her good hand as Frankie grabbed her arm and helped her to her feet. Together, they walked down the long corridor, climbing up and over the broken pieces of hallway and ceiling in their path. When they got close to the collapsed staircase at the end of the hall, Cas asked, "Do you think there's another way down?"

"Could be." The stairs that mirrored this set down the front hallway on the other side of the school were their best shot. If those were destroyed, their only other option would be the ones at the rear of the school—which meant going back toward the fire. *No, thanks.*

"Don't take offense, since this has nothing to do with you, but I didn't think I could hate this place more than I already did before."

"Then what are you doing here?" Frankie pitched a board obstructing his path to one side, shoved another, and then realized Cas hadn't answered. Turning, he asked, "You must have a pretty good reason for being here at school today."

"Does it matter?" she asked.

It didn't. But the way she was evading the question told him it should. So instead of dropping it, he said, "Humor me. School isn't in session. You aren't interested in being fashionable in polyester marching-band uniforms. You could have found someplace else to practice clarinet if you wanted to. So, why come? And why come up here?" It's not as if the art room she'd been stuck in was right around the corner from the music department, where he'd first spotted her. Far from it.

Cas hugged her bag to her chest. "The art room was

quiet, and I figured no one would notice me in there. Things have been . . ." She shrugged again. "I needed to get away." Before he could comment, she asked, "What about you? Why are you here instead of off doing whatever it is football players do?"

Frankie mentally ran through the path he'd taken to get here and the stops he'd made along the way and Tad, who had said his time was up just before the first bomb went off. He started to answer when he heard someone shouting.

"Do you hear that?" he asked.

Cas turned. "I think it's coming from down that way. Someone must need help."

It could be Tad.

"Let's go find out."

RASHID

– CHAPTER 30 –

"**THEY'RE DEAD.**"

One of them must have been alive only a few minutes ago. The call had been weak, but he'd heard it and followed the sound. If he'd only gotten here a few minutes earlier . . .

Nothing would have changed. Nothing he could have done would have saved them. Rashid smoothed the dead girl's sleeve. The pool of blood under her head ran along the cracks in the bathroom tile near where the other woman, Mrs. Barnes, lay on the floor. The two of them must have gotten caught in the bathroom when the bomb went off, or maybe Mrs. Barnes pulled the girl in here thinking it would be safer when the building started to come apart. The broken glass that had sliced the artery in Mrs. Barnes's neck showed how little was safe now.

Tad turned and stared down the hall. Rashid wished he could look away. But he couldn't. The stream of blood following the grout in between the tiles reached where he was kneeling, and still he didn't move.

Mrs. Barnes had taught history. Rashid had taken AP American History from her. He was supposed to have AP European History with her this year. She valued all her students equally and made sure they knew that every voice was important to the conversation in her class. He remembered when the discussion turned to the Japanese internment camps during World War II. She'd made sure the class knew it was never fair to condemn an entire racial group based on the actions of a few and had everyone in the room do a project on the time and place when their heritage was considered a threat.

He'd wished everyone in the school could take her class. She'd taught her students that if people took the time and effort, they'd still believe in what America pretended to stand for. She'd given him hope that maybe, just maybe, things would change if he just waited.

But nothing had gotten better, and he'd realized that waiting around for other people to change was pointless. If you wanted something to be different, you had to do it yourself. The beard was to have been his first step. A small but important test to see how others would react. How he would feel before forging down a path different from the one his father expected him to take.

"Come on. They're dead. There's nothing we can do." Tad stalked into the hallway, letting the door he'd been holding open close behind him.

Darkness wrapped around Rashid. He let it settle on him

for a moment before reaching for his phone. Using the glow, Rashid looked at the unfamiliar girl. She had long, dark hair that she wore tied back behind her neck, and deep brown skin. Her face must have been beautiful before today. The side of it that hadn't been smashed open still was.

Rashid turned away from the blood and gore that seemed even more horrifying in the dim light. He'd seen pictures of worse things that had happened in bombings in Palestine. In an effort to make him understand what it meant to really be a Muslim, his cousins had shown him places where people had died. They wanted him to feel what they thought he was supposed to feel. Sadness had walked the streets with him while his cousins had described the people who had been bombed as they shopped at a market. How could anyone see the scars on the streets and buildings and the wariness in the eyes of people trying to go about their lives and not feel their anxiety and fear?

He had wanted neither. But right now he was filled with both, in ways he had never felt on those streets. This blood was real. Mrs. Barnes and the girl were walking these halls an hour ago. They never knew they were supposed to be afraid. They didn't know they'd stayed too long at a place they had every right to believe was safe.

Until it was too late.

Slowly, Rashid wrapped his fingers around the dead girl's hand. He then reached out and put his other hand on Mrs. Barnes's shoulder.

Even though Rashid didn't know the girl, he felt the loss of the life that was cut short, one that he would now never have the chance to be a part of. She probably wouldn't have wanted to know him. She might have even called him names. But if she had, he forgave her.

He looked at both of them, then closed his eyes and quietly said, "I bear witness that there is no god but Allah." The words had to be said by a Muslim when dying. They were not meant to help those who did not believe in Islam, but Rashid felt the need to say the words anyway.

For them.

For himself. Because he had come into this school to do something to change his life. To find a way to be seen for more than his religion, to be a person who was more than just one thing. And this is what had happened.

Sitting back on his heels, Rashid said the words a second time, then prayed for forgiveness from Allah. The door to repentance was always open. Rashid had heard those words all his life, typically after he'd done something his parents disapproved of. Often he said "I'm sorry" because it was expected of him. Rarely did he mean it with his whole heart. Today he meant it down to his soul.

I'm sorry.

Shifting the light, Rashid looked at the girl again and spotted a small yellow bag sticking out from under one of her legs and slid it out. He unsnapped the flap of the purse and was rummaging through the zippered compartments when the door opened.

"What are you doing?" Tad appeared in the entrance. His body was framed by the faint light behind him, making him appear almost spirit-like. A shiver went up Rashid's neck.

"What does it matter to you?" Rashid asked, willing Tad to close the door and go away. "I thought you were going to find a way out."

"I was, but then I thought about that 911 call you didn't make and . . ." Tad crossed his arms over his chest and stood in the middle of the doorway. "I just wanted to see what you were doing."

"Because I might be planting a bomb in here?"

Tad tightened his arms over his chest.

"I'm looking for her ID!" The words shot like a bullet out of Rashid. "I want to be able to pray for her by name. She deserves for someone to know her name." He opened the purse and dug through the contents.

There was an open pack of gum. A wallet with money and pictures. A small, almost crumpled photo hidden in one pocket along with a half-eaten roll of mints. A set of keys on a fuzzy bee keychain. Pens. Earbuds. A bunch of receipts and other trash, and finally a school ID card with the girl's smiling face beaming from it.

"Angelica Johnson," he said, wishing the girl could still smile. "She was going to be a freshman this year."

Not someone who had called him names. Just a girl waiting for the next part of her life to start. And it was over.

"Now what are you doing?" Tad asked as Rashid closed his eyes.

Rashid didn't answer as he sent a silent prayer to Allah to take care of the teacher and young girl who should not have been caught in a war zone. Then Rashid pulled from her wallet the small, bent picture of her and two of her friends making stupid faces in a photo booth. He grabbed his bag and slid both the ID card and the photo into a side pocket.

"What did you take?"

That was it.

Rashid spun around. "What is wrong with you?" He dug back into the pocket, pulled out the ID card, and held it up. "Here. This is what I took. If we get out of here, I thought I could give it to the police. I thought . . ." He shook his head and raked a hand through his hair. Shrugging, he said, "I thought if I get out of here, I could let the emergency workers know where she died so they could find her and bring her back to her family. I thought her family might want to know what happened to her and that they might want her ID."

If she'd gotten the identification card today, it was the last photograph ever taken of her. Her family would want to see her last smile.

Rashid waited for Tad to say something horrible. When he didn't, Rashid slid the card back next to the photograph he planned on keeping for himself no matter what happened.

"Now where are you going?" Tad shouted as Rashid pushed past him out of the bathroom and back into the hall.

Turning, he looked Tad dead in the eye and said, "I'm going to look for a way out of the school. While I do that, feel free to check the bathroom for the bombs you seem to think I am setting. I'm sure that'll be a good use of your time and will keep you far away from me. And who knows? Maybe part of the ceiling will fall in and kill me. That would no doubt make you very happy."

Then, without looking back, Rashid strode down the hall to his right, around the wreckage, looking for a path that would get him as far away from Tad and his hate as possible. He was grateful to Tad for helping him get out of the bathroom he'd been trapped in. If not for Tad, he could have died exactly like Mrs. Barnes and Angelica had. But he was done letting the idiotic football player kick him over and over as if he were a dog. He wasn't a dog or a Moo-slim or any of the other names he'd been called by Tad and his friends over the years. He was just Rashid Farsoun, and all he'd ever wanted was a chance to live his life like everyone else did.

Carefully, he pushed aside wires with part of what he was assuming used to be a door frame so he could get closer to the collapsed staircase. Maybe the damage wasn't as bad as it looked from afar.

Fluorescent lights dangled from the ceiling. Water poured out of an exposed pipe on the far end of the hallway. There were broken beams and smashed ceiling tiles, but aside from the smoke that seemed to be drifting from the missing tiles in the ceiling, the damage here wasn't as bad as it was behind him.

At least not yet.

Rashid checked his phone. Still no signal.

Putting the phone back in his pocket, he continued down the hall. The smoke grew thicker and the temperature was getting warmer.

12:34 P.M.

TAD

— CHAPTER 31 —

"HEY," **TAD CALLED** as Rashid walked down the hazy hall. But Rashid didn't stop or look back.

Damn it all to hell. He should have just kept his mouth shut. But seeing more people dead had freaked him out. He hadn't meant . . . he didn't really think . . . He saw Rashid disappear around the corner and hurried after him.

"Hey. Wait up. I'm sorry. Okay? I didn't really think that you were planting a bomb." He just couldn't get the lie about the 911 call out of his head. And Rashid was hiding something.

"Really?" Rashid yelled without looking back. "Then what did you think I was doing in there? I'm pretty sure whatever you were thinking was terrible. But you want me to believe you're really a nice guy."

"I deserve that." He did. And worse. "Just wait up, okay?" He was breathless as he reached Rashid, who had stopped and turned. Waiting for whatever it was he had to say.

Only what could he say?

Damn. He shoved a locker shut. Metal slammed against

metal, making Rashid jerk, but he never took his eyes off Tad. Waiting for answers.

"Look," Tad blurted. "There was a friend I was supposed to meet today. And I'm not sure if he's still trapped in here." *Friend.* Not exactly the truth, but it was close enough. "I've been thinking about him ever since the first explosion, and then we found someone and they weren't alive, and it made me think . . ." Tad jammed his hands into his pockets and looked at the wet floor as the hollowness he'd felt when Rashid had announced the people inside the bathroom were dead returned. All the anger and frustration that had brought him here today had vanished in an instant when he thought Frankie might be one of them. He'd wanted Frankie to pay for hurting him, but now he wasn't so sure what he wanted. Just as he wasn't sure what Rashid wanted from him. He'd screwed up, but he wasn't the kind of person Rashid thought he was.

Tad could feel Rashid's eyes still on him. "I'm not . . ." He shrugged and kept his own eyes lowered. "I know my friends say a lot of things, but I never do. I'm not like them."

"Really? So you automatically assumed I had something to do with the bombing, but you aren't racist like they are? Fine. You can keep telling yourself that." Rashid shook his head and started walking again.

"I'm not a racist!" he yelled at Rashid's back. "Hey." He hurried after him. "You know I'm half black." Tad's footsteps were right behind Rashid.

"Wow. I never noticed." Rashid's laugh was bitter as he

stepped over a fallen board. "You think that means you're not a racist? Then why did you automatically assume I'm hiding something terrible because I didn't want to tell you who I called when I thought I was going to die?" Rashid stopped next to an open doorway.

"It's not because I'm a racist, and it isn't my fault my friends say crap things sometimes." Tad stopped walking. "You don't know anything about me, so don't pretend you know me."

Sweat trickled down his back. The hallway was growing hotter. The smoke was thicker, making it harder to breathe.

Rashid turned and started walking again. "You're right. I don't know a thing about you. But not knowing me didn't stop you from passing judgment." Rashid rounded the corner. "Your double standard is—"

Rashid suddenly went quiet. Tad raced around the corner and almost crashed right into Rashid, who was standing as still as a rock. Then Tad looked beyond Rashid and realized why.

Smoke. Waves of it poured down the stairs located smack in the middle of the hallway. Dark tendrils were coming from the blackened ceiling. And there were flames.

"Aw, hell!" Tad looked back down the hallway they had just come from and then toward the staircase in the middle of the hallway . . . near the fire. "This sucks. This really and completely sucks."

Rashid didn't move. He was just staring straight ahead as if he'd fallen into some kind of trance. *Great.* This was just perfect.

Tad stepped around Rashid, swallowed down the pulsing panic, and rubbed the back of his sweat-coated neck. The fire hadn't reached this floor yet. It was still in the upper stairwell. The stairwell going down looked okay. But who knew how long that would last?

"Screw it. I'm going."

"What are you doing?" Rashid asked, grabbing his arm. "You could get burned. We should wait for the firefighters to put out the fire."

"If we wait, the fire will spread to the rest of the staircase." He pulled his arm out of Rashid's grasp and started down the hall, trying hard to ignore how much hotter the air was with every step. "I lost one escape route because I decided to save you. I'm not going to lose another."

"And what about the friend you said was still in the school?" Rashid called. "Do you intend on leaving him to die?"

Tad turned. "I don't even know for sure that he was in the school when the bombs went off. He probably stood me up."

The heat pushed like a stiff wind, stealing the air around him.

Pressure built in his chest.

He wiped his stinging eyes and turned back toward the stairs. The fire was moving down them, closer to the second-floor landing, but the stairs going down to the first story were still clear of flames. "I think we can make it."

The smoke was terrifying. Flames crackled as they licked the stairs, getting closer to their level. Tad started forward, but

Rashid grabbed Tad's arm and yanked him back. Tad stumbled and slipped on the wet floor.

"Let me go."

"Stop."

"We can make it if we go now."

"Just stop."

"You want to stay here, fine, but I'm going."

"Wait!"

Rashid's fingers dug into Tad's arm and refused to let go.

"Look in that locker!" Rashid yelled, pointing through the growing haze toward the wall near the stairwell.

"Who cares about a locker? We can—" That's when Tad saw what Rashid was pointing at. A flicker of red light glowing near the bottom of one of the lockers.

He squinted and took a step forward to get a better look as a wave of hot air swept over him. Sweat dripped down his back. "What the hell is that?"

Something in the stairwell above snapped and cracked, and a flaming board crashed down the stairs.

Rashid grabbed his arm and pulled hard, but Tad held his ground as he studied the stairs. He could still make it. He was fast. If he went now, he might get down to the first floor. Then he looked back at the locker, squinted into the haze, and realized what the red glow was. Numbers. And they were counting down.

"Tad! Run!"

Holy hell.

Something cracked.

The fire roared down the stairs.

Tad took two steps backwards, then turned and followed Rashid's lead. He ran.

"This way!" Rashid shouted over his shoulder as something else came crashing down in the stairwell. Tad ran faster. He couldn't breathe. Rashid rounded the corner. Tad raced right behind him. The minute the flames reached that locker, all bets were—

Z

— CHAPTER 32 —

"**Screw them!** They have to come help." Z slid his head and one arm out the narrow window and waved at the people standing at the parking lot far in the distance. "Hey. Yo! We need help. Hello! It's time to do your freakin' jobs. Are you blind?"

"They see you," Diana said as he craned his neck to get a better view of the parking lot and the dozens of people in uniforms who were standing in the hot sun, looking up at the building while gesturing and shouting but essentially doing nothing. *Nothing!*

"Look over there," Diana called to him. He looked down to where she pointed, farther to the right, where people in dark blue jackets were standing at the base of the north set of steps, which led up to the front entrance. On the back of the jackets were stamped the letters FBI.

"Hey!" he screamed down at them. "Move your asses and get us out of here!"

Still they didn't budge. *Damn it!*

"You might as well stop screaming," Diana said. "They aren't going to pay attention to you."

"Well, it's not like we have a hell of a lot of other choices," he said, kicking the wall beneath the window. Diana was right. Between the sirens and the people shouting and the helicopters whirring overhead, there was no chance anyone could hear him. Still, standing around doing nothing wasn't an option.

"Let me try," she said as she unlatched the narrow window at her end of the room and cranked it until it opened as far as it would go. There was a safety feature that was supposed to keep kids from doing something stupid—like jumping. Or being able to scream for help during a bombing.

Still, Diana managed to get her arm through. She looked up at the sky instead of down at the ground then waved her arms and said, "Please. We need help."

"If they couldn't hear me, do you think they're actually going to hear you?" Z sneered.

"It's not about hearing me!" she shouted at him before waving toward the sky and calling up again.

Good, Z thought, because the whirring sound of a chopper grew louder, drowning out anything she had to say.

Slowly, she twisted enough to pull her head and arm back inside, then raced across the room.

"What the hell are you doing?" Z asked as she ripped a poster of the Eiffel Tower off a bulletin board and flipped it over. "This isn't the time to make paper airplanes."

"I need a marker. They can't hear us, but there's a camera on that news helicopter."

A camera that could see a message and let the people on the ground know that Kaitlin needed help.

"I'll find something." Z hurried toward the desk at the front of the room near Kaitlin. He glanced over at her as he threw open a drawer. "Hang in there, Kaitlin. Diana's got a good idea to get us out of here." He pulled out the next drawer and felt a surge of triumph. "Will this work?" he yelled.

Diana turned, and he tossed the thick, dark red marker over to her. She caught it and nodded. "It's perfect!"

She brushed off a desk, flipped the poster over, and started writing. Z squeezed Kaitlin's hand, then crossed the room to read Diana's message.

I'M DIANA SANFORD. MY FATHER IS SENATOR HOWARD SANFORD. THE EXITS ARE BLOCKED. WE NEED HELP.

"What the hell?" Z grabbed the poster off the desk. "What about me and Kaitlin? You didn't even mention that she's injured and needs help right now. Don't you think they should know that?"

"Nothing I write about Kaitlin is going to make a difference."

"But telling them your name will? News flash. If we die, you're going to die too. It doesn't matter who your daddy is."

"Don't you think I know that?" She grabbed the sign and

headed for the window. "The media cares about a school getting bombed and people getting trapped inside, but they care more when a United States senator's daughter is fighting for her life with no one making a move to help get her out."

"That's stupid."

"Maybe," she said, sliding the poster through the open window. "But that doesn't make it less true. I didn't make the rules."

He balled his hand into a fist and stalked to the other window as Diana angled the poster up toward the sky so the camera she promised was on board would get a shot of it when the chopper flew by. Poking his head through the window, Z waved his arms to help get attention. "Hey! We're here. Read the stupid sign and come help us."

The news chopper flew closer, and Z craned his neck to look up at it. Then he glanced down at the parking lot, where the emergency workers continued to hold their ground.

This was a bust.

"Okay, Princess," Z said, pulling his head back inside. "They saw your stupid sign. And they still aren't coming in."

Ducking back inside, Diana said, "We have to be patient. They have to follow protocol."

"Protocol can kiss my—"

"Hello?"

"What was that?" Z whirled toward the door.

"Hello?" the voice came again, and Z let out a whoop.

"Kaitlin, do you hear that? They're coming." Firefighters were coming to the rescue. They were going to get out of this.

"You're going to be okay." Z wove through desks and yelled back, "Hey! We're down here. There's someone injured in here."

"Hello?" the voice called out again. This time closer.

"Please hurry." Z knelt down next to Kaitlin. Gently, he took her hand. She looked up at him, and he smiled as someone called, "Cas, they're here."

"Thank God you found us." Z looked toward the open doorway and stopped smiling. Standing there was a dirt-streaked, sweaty Frankie Ochoa. Not a firefighter who could help Kaitlin, but a football player with no way out—just like them.

DIANA

— CHAPTER 33 —

DIANA WASN'T SURE how to feel about Frankie's appearance. He was shirtless, and his tanned chest was covered with sweat and dust, a change from the last time they'd seen each other.

Two dates. He didn't show for the third, and he never bothered to tell her why. She refused to ask and instead took it as a sign. Now he was here, and the horror on Z's face made it clear how he felt about seeing the star quarterback.

"It's you." Z glanced behind Frankie as if hoping for someone else to appear.

And someone did.

Her face looked almost gray next to her dark frizzy hair. Her eyes were wide and glassy. Dirt and blood smeared the girl's face and neck. It looked as if she had one arm wrapped in a dirty sling.

"I can tell I'm not exactly who you were hoping to see,"

Frankie said, looking at Diana. His eyes flicked up at the hole in the ceiling and then swept over the massive metal air conditioner wedged into the floor. Frankie went completely still and the cocky smile he always seemed to be wearing disappeared as he spotted Kaitlin under it.

"Oh, God," the girl with the bandaged arm said. "Is she dead?"

"Not yet," Kaitlin answered for herself.

"Not at all." Z knelt down next to her. "Once the firefighters decide to do their job, we'll get you out of here."

"What are you talking about?" Frankie asked.

"Look outside." Z pointed toward the window he'd shattered. "The firefighters and police and everyone are just waiting around out there for the building to collapse. They aren't doing anything."

"That makes no sense," said the girl with the sling as Frankie hopped over a desk and followed Z to the window. While Frankie yelled and waved at the people below—because clearly he believed she and Z must not have done it right in the first place—the new girl asked, "What are they waiting for? An invitation?"

"Little Miss Princess here gave them one. She seemed to think they'd trip over themselves to help if they knew she was in the building." Z sneered. "Must sting to know they care just as little about you as they do about the rest of us."

It would if it were true.

"I guarantee you that dozens of politicians are on the phone right now demanding action and threatening anyone who will listen with hearings and investigations to make something happen."

"And yet nothing's happening," Z said, kneeling down next to Kaitlin, who had started to cough. "Kaitlin needs help now."

"And I told you, they must think there are more bombs," Diana said. She walked to the window. "Look at how far back everyone is standing." She took her phone out of her pocket and said, "I don't have cell service. Does anyone else?"

Frankie pulled his out and frowned. "You think they turned it off?"

"But that would mean they don't want us to be able to use our phones to call for help. They wouldn't do that," said the new girl Diana had almost forgotten about.

"Yeah—they would." Frankie shoved his hands in his pockets. The cockiness that Frankie was known for and that Diana once found fascinating—until she realized he wasn't as confident as he pretended to be—was gone. "Because they think there could be more bombs."

"Well, I don't know about you, but I'm not waiting around for the people out there to get their crap together." Z grabbed the long board he'd pitched to the ground earlier. "I'm getting this thing off of Kaitlin, and I'm finding a way out of this place."

He shoved the board under the side of the air conditioner that was pinning Kaitlin's legs down. It wasn't going to work, but Diana found herself almost hoping it would as she said, "Wait a second. Before you do anything, let's find bandages so we can make a tourniquet for her legs when we pull her out. She's going to hemorrhage, and we have to stop that as fast as possible or she'll die before we ever have the chance to leave this room."

Frankie nodded. "She's right. See what you can find in this room. I'll check the ones down the hall." He turned toward the dark-haired girl and said, "Hang here, Cas. I'll be right back."

Frankie gave Cas's shoulder a gentle squeeze, then hurried out of the room. He ignored Diana, and she didn't care. Frankie wasn't anything more than a guy she had kissed twice. No big deal. Right now, none of that mattered, she told herself as she did a slow turn, taking in everything that was in the room.

Z was rummaging through the teacher's desk. Cas was still clutching her bag close to her while leaning on the door frame as she looked down the hall—probably watching for Frankie, just like every other girl at this school.

"We could use the straps of your bag," Diana said to Cas. "We can use them to tourniquet Kaitlin's legs and try to stop them from bleeding."

"Good." Z slammed a drawer shut, making Cas jump.

Kaitlin remained still as a stone. "Because there's nothing in here to use. Here, give it to me."

Cas stepped backwards into the doorway, shifting so Z couldn't grab her bag.

"Over my dead body," the girl shot back. She looked as if she might collapse at any minute, but she still had fight left in her and tugged the bag back toward her—surprising Z, who let go. He started to reach for it again, and the girl almost tripped going backwards through the door as Frankie called, "I've got something."

He appeared behind Cas, juggling several rolls of duct tape and a bunch of paper towels. "There's a lot of smoke coming down the hall. Once we get Kaitlin free, we're going to have to find a way down to the first floor and out of here—fast."

Diana kept her eyes on Cas as Frankie stepped into the room and started explaining how the bandaging would work once Kaitlin was free. Cas leaned against the doorway again and looked down at the bag she was hugging against her chest.

"Whatever's in that bag must really be important," Diana said quietly as the boys circled the air conditioner, discussing their options.

Cas didn't respond, and her dark hair was hanging in front of her face, so Diana couldn't see what she might be thinking. She just clutched the bag tighter, making Diana really wonder what was inside.

"Diana, could you come help us?" Frankie yelled.

Cas's bag would wait.

Turning, she asked, "What do you want me to do?"

"You're going to pull Kaitlin out once the air conditioner is lifted," Frankie told her. "We won't be able to hold it very long."

"Give me the tape and the paper towels and a sec to get ready." Trying not to look at Kaitlin's pale face, Diana ripped several long strips of duct tape off the roll with her teeth and hung them from the leg of an overturned chair. She then stacked paper towels nearby.

"Here," Z said, pulling his shirt over his head and tossing it to her. "You can use this, too."

"Okay," she said, putting her hands under Kaitlin's slight shoulders and wishing she wasn't in charge of this part. But it wasn't as if Cas was up to the challenge.

"Are you ready, Kaitlin?" Z asked. Kaitlin clenched her teeth, shut her eyes tightly, and nodded as Z wedged his board in the space between the floor and the metal near the end of the air conditioner. He stood on one side, while Frankie stood on the other. They set themselves, and Frankie yelled, "Here we go. One. Two. Three."

The guys grunted and pushed down on the lever. The box edged up. Diana dug her fingers into Kaitlin's armpits and held her breath as it moved again. Then she pulled.

Kaitlin screamed, and Diana almost let go. Kaitlin was still being crushed. The boys groaned, and the box edged up a fraction of an inch more. Diana tugged again. Kaitlin let out another yelp as Diana pulled her backwards.

"She's free!" Frankie yelled as the air conditioner crashed back to the ground. He quickly helped Diana wrap Z's shirt and paper towels around her legs while Z bound the makeshift bandages with duct tape.

"Now, does anyone have an idea of how we can get out of here?" Frankie asked.

"We could go back down the way I came up," Diana said, trying not to look at Kaitlin's injuries as they worked. But it was hard not to. There was some blood coming from a puncture in one of her thighs, but not as much blood as Diana had feared there would be. Still, the shape and odd angle of both of Kaitlin's legs made it clear the damage inside them was severe. Frankie wrapped ripped pieces of T-shirt and paper towels around the puncture wound to stop the bleeding, then told Diana to look for something they could use for splints.

"I've got it," Z said, grabbing two pieces of splintered two-by-fours off the ground before Diana had a chance to move.

Every second that Frankie and Z spent winding duct tape around the splints felt like an hour.

Diana checked the time on her phone and shoved it back into her pocket.

Hurry up, she thought. They had to hurry up if they were going to get—

A loud boom shook the building. As Frankie shoved her to the floor, all Diana could think was that they were too late, as somewhere a third bomb was exploding.

12:41 P.M.

TAD

— CHAPTER 34 —

THERE WAS A FLASH, and everything exploded.

Tad slammed to the floor.

Metal lockers flew open.

The ceiling fell from above.

He put his arms over his face. A blast of heat seared his skin and his lungs as he inhaled the scorching air. Somewhere, someone screamed. There was another rumble, and the screaming stopped.

His heart leaped into his throat, and he scrambled to his knees. A hand appeared in front of his face. He didn't think twice before grabbing it and letting Rashid haul him up. Together, they bolted down the side hallway. The shaking floor made them stumble, but they stayed on their feet and raced back to the side of the school where they'd come from.

It wasn't until they reached the end of the next hall, near one of the collapsed stairwells, that they stopped running. Tad's lungs were on fire. He gulped air, and when he coughed, he tasted soot. His ears rang. Beside him, Rashid sank to the floor and put his head in his hands.

And that's when it hit Tad. Rashid might not like him, but he had made sure Tad had gotten out of harm's way. It was hard to believe that someone who was involved with this would have cared if he'd gotten caught in the blast. Not that Tad had really thought Rashid was behind any of this. Not really. He just wished Rashid had told him who he had called.

Tad shook the ringing out of his ears and pushed the thought to the side. All he really knew was that they were back where they had started. Still stuck in this hellhole, with God only knew how many more bombs ready to go off at any minute.

"If we get out of this, I owe you for saving my life." Tad's throat burned. The water dripping in the distance taunted him. He would sell a piece of his soul for a drink of cold water.

Rashid slowly rose to his feet. He frowned as he looked up and down the hall as if searching for something.

"The smoke's getting thicker," Tad said, breaking the silence.

Finally, Rashid said, "I think we should find a fire extinguisher."

Tad laughed. "You think a fire extinguisher is going to put out that?" He pointed down the hall at the black smoke billowing their way. "Are you crazy?"

"Yes." Rashid turned and started down the hall, away from the smoke. "I thought you already had that figured out."

Yeah. He'd earned that.

Tad shot one last look down the hall in the direction of the fire, then followed Rashid, who had found the fire extinguisher in this part of the school.

Rashid grabbed a thick piece of wood and smashed it against the fire-extinguisher case. The glass shattered, but he cocked back and took another swing at it before dropping the wood. Finally, he yanked the extinguisher from the holder and took several deep breaths.

"Feel better?" Tad asked with a smile.

Rashid looked down at the fire extinguisher in his hands then the shattered glass on the floor among the rest of the wreckage and shocked the hell out of Tad when he flashed a grin. "Yeah. I do."

"So," Tad asked again, "what's the plan? It's not like we can climb out a window and jump."

Not from the second story, which was technically three stories up from the sidewalk because of the school's design. Even if they managed to squeeze themselves through the narrow windows, they would have to drop thirty feet or more to concrete and brick below. If they could get to the east side of the building, they could jump onto the grass, but that part of the school was currently on fire.

Breaking a leg on the concrete would be better than burning to death, but there was also a good chance he'd split his head open. "Do you have a plan other than holding a fire extinguisher and hoping for the best?" Tad repeated.

"Yes," Rashid answered. "I plan on using the pressure in the fire extinguisher to propel us from the school like a jetpack. How about you test it first?"

Tad stared at Rashid, who shook his head, then laughed. "I'm joking."

"You're joking?" Tad didn't know the guy even knew how to joke, and here he was doing it with the building coming down around their heads.

"The smoke is getting worse, which is probably more dangerous right now than the fire. I think we should barricade ourselves in one of the rooms as far away from the fire as we can get and wait there until help arrives," Rashid said, all traces of laughter gone.

"So we just sit around and wait for the fire or another bomb to kill us?" This plan left a lot to be desired.

"Do you have a better idea?"

He would give anything to say yes. "No, but . . ." He cocked his head to the side and held up his hand. "Listen. Do you hear something?"

"Hear what?"

He looked around and waited for the sound to come again.

"Is anyone down there?"

Voices. People were calling. The voices were muffled.

"Hello?" Tad yelled back. Then he turned to Rashid. "I think the voices are coming from above. Maybe the firefighters or the cops are here after all. Come on." He thought he heard someone shout back, but the sound was too faint to make out the words. "Can you tell where they are?"

Rashid shook his head. "Maybe somewhere closer to the middle of the hall? It's hard to say. Hello? Are you there?" he shouted, then froze as he listened.

Tad held his breath as he waited for the voices to come again. "That way," he said. He ignored the smoke that was billowing around the corner as he sprinted down the hall. Rashid followed, trying door handles along the way.

"This one is open," Rashid said as he pulled. A desk crashed through the opening. Everything inside the room creaked. Debris rained on top of Rashid. Tad bolted forward, grabbed Rashid's arms, and pulled him out of the way.

"You okay?" He coughed, then squatted down next to Rashid.

"Never better," Rashid said as he wiped at the blood streaming from a cut on his face. Tad started to unbutton his shirt to use as a bandage, but Rashid was already tearing a piece of his own shirt away and pressing it to his head. When Tad moved to help, Rashid leaned back. "I'm fine."

Tad heard the voices again, which sounded as if they were coming from the open doorway. "Hello?" he yelled, peering through a gap in the wreckage wedged in the doorway to see into the room beyond.

Holy destruction, Batman.

The place was a mess of twisted metal and busted boards and pieces of wall or ceiling. Here and there, he could see streaks of light snaking through a haze of smoke. "Hey?" Tad shouted again. "Anyone?"

Please. Let the firefighters be there.

"Do you hear that?" a male voice shouted from above. "I think someone's down there."

"Yes!" Tad coughed and choked out, "There are two of us down here on the second floor." He turned to look at Rashid, who was staggering to his feet, still pressing the shirt to his head. Blood was smeared across the side of his face. "Do you hear that, Rashid? We're going to get the hell out of here! They're coming to save us."

"There are five of us up here on the third," someone else called, and Tad's breath caught in his throat. He knew that voice.

It wasn't a firefighter coming to help them escape. The voice belonged to Frankie. He hadn't left the building and ditched Tad after all. And now he was here.

FRANKIE

– CHAPTER 35 –

FRANKIE'S CHEST TIGHTENED. He recognized the voice coming from below. Still, he found himself asking, "Tad is that you?"

"Yeah, Frankie. It's me. Guess this is life's way of telling me I should have gone to the team party after all. Right?"

Frankie's heart leaped, even as he tensed. Whatever had been between them for those few weeks was over. Done. It should never even have started—whatever it was. And what was happening now didn't change any of that.

He looked back at Z holding Kaitlin. Diana and Cas were not far behind them. They were ready to climb down to the floor below.

"We're all going to work together to get out of this," he called, deliberately keeping his tone businesslike and hoping Tad would pick up the cue. "But first we have to get down by you."

"There's a lot of smoke down here, the stairways are blocked, and the east side of the school is on fire. Maybe we should try to come up and get to the roof. I could swear I heard helicopters."

"The third floor is in bad shape. Part of the roof is caved in. There's no way we can get to the door for the roof." *Or through it.* The door was steel and they kept it locked, for obvious reasons. "Things might suck down there, but at least you're closer to the ground. That has to give us more options."

"Are we going down there, or are we going to talk until the building collapses around us?" Z asked.

Frankie shot Z an annoyed look, then turned and stared down into the destruction that was the room below them. From here it was impossible to see the door, which didn't bode well. "We're coming down now," he called to Tad.

"The door has broken desks and shelves and other stuff wedged into it. I could try to clear some of the stuff from the entryway, but anything I move could make other wreckage inside the room shift. That could make things worse."

Frankie took a look back at Kaitlin, who was whimpering in pain. "We're going to have to risk it. Just let me know when you're doing something that could send things flying. Okay?"

"Sure thing."

"Okay," he said, grabbing on to a metal bar hanging near the doorway he was standing in. "I'll go first and spot you guys on the way down."

"Don't worry about me," Diana said, locking eyes with him. "You should focus on people who need your help."

He saw anger flash across Diana's face for just a second before it vanished into an expression of concern. "Kaitlin and Cas need you, and I've already climbed this one. I know what I'm doing."

"Be careful," Cas said as she appeared behind Z.

"I'll do my best," Frankie promised, scoping out what looked like the best path for all of them and starting downward.

"There's no moving this desk that's wedged into the doorway," Tad called from below. "I think I can move stuff underneath it without causing anything else to fall, but there's a hell of a lot of smoke and a big-ass fire heading this way. So whatever you want to do to get down here, you're going to want to do it quick, or you might get singed."

I might get singed no matter how fast I climb, Frankie thought as he worked his way downward, trying not to grab on to anything that would injure his hands.

"Z," Frankie called when he reached a fairly stable desktop about a third of the way down, "pass Kaitlin to me. Then you can climb down here and we can work on getting her the rest of the way."

He'd been amazed that Kaitlin hadn't been gushing blood when Diana pulled her free from the air conditioner. But he still had no idea if they could get her down the wreckage to the next floor without hurting her worse. The splints were holding, and with Diana's help, Z had managed to keep her legs mostly steady and elevated on the trip down the hall. But this was going to be a hell of a lot harder.

They'd move the ball down the field step by step until they got to the end zone. If nothing else, they had to try.

It was touch-and-go. Kaitlin could barely keep her arms around Z's neck, which meant the guy had no hands to grab anything to help him make the climb down. Not with one hand under Kaitlin's knees and the other keeping her tight against his chest. Every time she whimpered, Z looked as if he wanted to punch out a window.

The smoke was getting thicker as Frankie helped Cas make the descent. He heard Diana start down after them, but he kept his eyes firmly on Cas as she bit her lip and tried not to show how scared she was that she was going to lose her grip and fall.

"You okay?" he asked when Cas was about halfway to the floor.

"In my next life, I'm coming back as a mountain goat."

He'd heard worse ideas.

Frankie caught a glimpse of Tad talking to someone on the other side of the debris that jammed the doorway as he helped Cas reach the bottom. Z worked on sliding Kaitlin through the space under one of the wedged desks into the hall.

Kaitlin moaned, and Z frowned as he shouted to Tad, "Do you have her? You have to be careful of her legs."

"Yeah. She's through. We're going to take her into one of the classrooms where there's less smoke. We'll be back in a minute."

Good, Frankie thought, but they weren't going to wait.

Frankie turned to Z. "One of us should go first and the other one last so we have someone on either side to help Cas and Diana through. Do you want to flip a coin?"

He could tell Z wanted to get to the other side to where Kaitlin was. He expected him to insist on going first, which was fine with Frankie. The more buffer he had between him and Tad when they finally were face-to-face, the better.

"You're smaller than me," Z said. "You'll get through faster. Just make sure nothing happens to Kaitlin before I get to the other side."

Well, hell.

"Okay, then."

The fit was tight, and the sweat on Frankie's back made him stick to the floor as he pushed himself along with his feet. He closed his eyes as dust from above showered down on top of him, and he winced as something scraped his skin. He shoved with his feet again and wriggled his hips to move several more inches. And then again until finally he opened his eyes and saw a hand appear in front of his face.

He looked at its long, brown fingers for a minute before taking it and letting Tad haul him to his feet.

"I'm out," Frankie called and started to step toward the doorway to help Cas, but Tad's fingers squeezed his arm tight as Tad quietly said, "Nice of you to finally drop by. I've been waiting."

Things do not change; we change.

—Henry David Thoreau

12:48 P.M.

CAS

— CHAPTER 36 —

DYING WOULD HAVE BEEN easier than this.

Her arm throbbed. Her head spun from the pain and the smoke and the tears she'd refused to let fall during the climb down or when Frankie had insisted she climb through that hole after he did. Even if her arm hadn't been injured, the hole would have been hard for her to squeeze through. With her arm injured—she had taken one look at the opening Frankie was pulling himself through and shaken her head. She wasn't going to make it through that space. Diana would, no problem. But Diana had insisted on climbing down last. She didn't need help. Not like Cas did. Diana could save herself.

Well, all the carrot and celery sticks her mother had given her for lunch mocked Cas as Frankie finished pulling himself through the gap and yelled that it was her turn. He would help her from the other side. Z was going to help from the rear.

That was the last thing she wanted.

She hugged her bag tight against her and thought about the gun inside.

"I know this isn't a news flash, but I'm hurt," Cas had said, backing up against a . . . She had no idea what it was she was leaning against. "It's going to take a while for me to get through, so Diana and Z should go before me. It's not fair to make them wait." And then they wouldn't have to see her struggle to get through the opening she knew wasn't large enough.

"I got Kaitlin through. You'll make it, Cas," Z promised as, from somewhere above, Diana kicked something that rattled down the piles of broken desks to the ground. "Put your injured arm through first, and I'll help guide you out."

"You can make it Cas," Frankie said from the other side. "Think snake-like thoughts, and you'll be fine. Trust me."

Trust him?

She wanted to. And she really didn't want to stay in here alone. She'd wanted to die alone before when it had been her choice. Now she was choosing to live, and she wasn't going to let this stupid school beat her. Not this time.

"Come on, Cas," Frankie said.

The smoke made her cough.

Fine. Be a snake.

Cas unfastened the sling from around her neck and winced as she slid her injured arm through the opening. She twisted and turned and grimaced at the pain while squeezing her chest through the gap in the doorway. Then she tried to pull the rest of herself through. When she got stuck, she knew her mother was wrong. Things weren't worse in her mind. There was nothing worse than being in massive pain and stuck in the only path to possible escape because you were too big to fit through the hole others had already gone through.

Panic bubbled. Heat flooded her face. Tears swam in her eyes because she was stuck and Z was now looking at her thighs and her butt and the way they were wedged in the opening that he needed to get through in order to live. She was stuck because she wasn't thin and athletic like her father had tried to convince her she needed to be.

She took a deep breath, wriggled her hips, and moved another inch as Frankie squatted down and yelled for Z to grab the desk and pull it up on the count of three.

Frankie put his hands under her armpits.

"One."

She bit her lip.

"Two."

Cas held her breath.

"Three."

The desk above her moved just a fraction of an inch, sending a bunch of other things flying, and Frankie pulled her free.

She'd made it. She was through.

Frankie helped her to her feet and pointed down the hazy, smoke-filled hall to a classroom.

"We're going to hole up in there until help arrives," said a guy wearing a dirty tux shirt next to Frankie. "My friend is in there with the injured girl."

Frankie nodded. "Go ahead, Cas. We'll all be there in a minute."

A backpack was coming through the hole, followed by Diana's head, as Cas turned and made for Mrs. Radke's chemistry room.

Some of the tables in the room were overturned. There was a haze of smoke and a lot of dust and books on the floor, but the room was in better condition than most of the school. Kaitlin was lying across two chemistry tables that had been pushed together, and a boy Cas didn't know was quietly talking to her while checking her pulse.

"Is she still okay?"

The boy glanced up at her, and she could see the answer in his eyes. "Her legs are crushed, and I think she's in shock. She really needs a doctor."

People were always going into shock on TV shows, but Cas couldn't remember what they did when it happened.

The boy clasped and unclasped his hands. "For shock, the doctors would normally raise her legs and keep her warm, but I think it's already too warm for her. And raising her legs might do more harm than good. Could you stay with her while I run to the classroom down the hall? I think Mr. Lott might have a stash of bottled water. She needs fluids."

The boy raced out of the room, almost knocking Diana over as she came in, holding a backpack that she hadn't been carrying when they were on the third floor. Diana walked over to one of the windows to see what was happening outside. A minute later, Z burst through the door with Frankie and the boy in the tux shirt right behind.

"Where's Rashid?" Tux-Shirt Guy asked.

Cas realized he was talking about the boy who had been helping Kaitlin. "He went to a room down the hall to get water."

"That's good," Z said as he went to take Kaitlin's hand. "We have to figure out a way to get Kaitlin out of here."

The injured girl was small, and despite the slight rise and fall of her chest, she looked dead.

Cas turned her back on the girl as the others huddled around Kaitlin's incredibly still body and moved toward the open windows, wishing she were anywhere else but here. Looking out, she could see more fire trucks arriving and being directed toward the back of the school.

"They must be trying to get the fire under control," Frankie said, slapping the tuxedo guy on the back. "Once they put out the fire and the bomb squad gives the all clear, they'll be able to get us out of here. We just have to hang tight, and it'll all be okay. Right, Tad?"

Tad shrugged off Frankie's hand as Z said, "Did you hear that, Kaitlin? It's almost over. We're going to get you out of here. You just have to hang on."

Maybe the worst was over. Cas turned and smiled at Diana, but she didn't seem to notice. Her eyes were fixed on the emergency workers climbing the steps to the entrance below—getting ready to come through the front doors. So Cas watched them too. If they were going to be rescued, then tomorrow really was going to come, and she wasn't sure how she was going to face it.

"I have water." They all turned toward the doorway, where Rashid was juggling a twelve-pack of water bottles.

"We think firefighters are coming in," Tad said as he turned away from the window. "We just have to wait, and it'll all be—"

The cracking boom sent Cas to the ground as the building once again began to shake. Pain flared in her arm. Tears welled as outside the window, people screamed. Kaitlin moaned, and Z held her hand between both of his.

This was bad.

No. Things were already bad. This was worse, she thought, pushing up with her good arm while her injured one felt as if it were on fire. Her heart stalled, then stormed in her chest. Another bomb had gone off just when they thought they were going to be rescued. "They targeted the firefighters," she whispered.

"You okay, Cas?" Frankie asked. "Is everyone okay?"

Tad and Diana both called out that they were unharmed. Rashid said he was fine too, but nothing was fine, Cas thought as she coughed and shook off Frankie's attempt to help her sit up.

Smoke billowed into the room, and she coughed again. Were the firefighters still fighting the fire? Could they?

"The bomb," Cas said, getting to her knees. "It must have been set off because the firefighters tried to come in and help us. And there could be more bombs." Four had gone off so far. How many could be somewhere, just waiting to explode? How soon before the fire reached the survivors trapped in this room or before they breathed in too much smoke? "Close the door," she called, but Rashid must have had the same thought, because he was already slamming it shut.

"Tad!" he yelled. "Help me wet down some paper towels and shove them under the door to block out the smoke."

The two worked side by side, with Tad wetting the paper towels and Rashid shoving them under the door until the smoke coming in was less noticeable.

"It would also help if we opened a window," Rashid said.

"But won't letting oxygen in feed the fire?" Cas asked, looking out at the chaos of several injured firefighters being carried to one of the ambulances in the visitors' parking lot.

"Breathing in smoke will be even worse," Rashid said. "Especially for Kaitlin."

Z didn't have to be told twice. He slid over a chemistry table and headed for a window while Frankie made a beeline for the other one. A minute later, the latches were flipped and the windows were opened as far as they would go. Which wasn't all that far, but it was better than nothing.

Or not, since Z stepped back and kicked hard at the window, making them all jump.

"What are you doing?" Cas asked.

"Trying to break the arm on this thing to open it farther.

If the firefighters aren't coming in to get us, we have to rescue ourselves."

"Kicking isn't going to break that thing," Frankie said at the same time Cas asked, "You want us to go out the window?"

The three windows in the room were narrow. It would be a tight squeeze for any of them, aside from Diana and Kaitlin, to fit through. And that was the least of their problems, considering there weren't any trees to jump to—not that Cas would actually be able to do that. Even if she were the athletic type, she'd never be able to grab hold of anything with a strong enough grip to keep her from splattering against the concrete below. It had to be at least twenty-five feet up from here to there. People in movies survived that kind of jump, but that didn't mean anyone would in real life.

"We can't jump," Tad shot back. "That would be suicide."

Hooray for the voice of reason.

"I'd rather jump and take my chances with the concrete than die up here doing nothing," Z shot back. "If I widen the window, we can hang from the ledge before dropping to the ground. The drop will be shorter."

Not enough to make a difference. The drop . . . the cement and brick below them . . . Even with a fire burning and the chance of more explosions, it wasn't a good option. Still, Z wasn't giving up. He rammed his shoulder against one of the open windows and grunted as the frame shuddered but didn't break.

"Kaitlin can't make that drop," Cas quietly said. "She'll die if you try."

Z spun toward Cas. Anger burned on his face.

"You can leave me, Z," Kaitlin said, her eyes fluttering open. Cas had thought the girl was unconscious. Clearly, she'd just been conserving her strength. "If you can get out of here, you should go. I don't want you to die. Your mother wouldn't have wanted you to do this."

"We both know whose fault this is. I was the one who was pissed at this place and wanted to let them know it. You're not going down because of me."

"Z . . ." Kaitlin panted hard, winced, and closed her eyes.

"No one is going down if we can help it," Frankie said as Z looked ready to beat the heck out of something. "We might not have come to this stupid school together, but we're all here now and we have to work as a team. Right, Tad?"

Frankie looked expectantly at Tad. Only Tad didn't agree. He just stared at Frankie as the silence stretched and tension Cas didn't understand crackled between them.

Finally, Frankie said, "The firefighters have to still be fighting the fire, but who knows when they'll be allowed to try to come back in the building."

Cas looked at Tad, who had turned away from Frankie before moving to one of the windows. She angled herself so she could see the far end of the building as Frankie continued, "We need to come up with a plan that will get us out of here. I don't know about all of you, but I'd rather not jump. If this were the gym, we'd have dozens of ropes and mats to use to lower Kaitlin to the ground, and the rest of us could climb to safety."

"Too bad chemistry teachers don't keep a stash of mats and ropes handy just in case of emergency," Z sneered. "Otherwise we'd be set."

"You're the one who said you wanted to get out of here, so maybe you should listen instead of being a jerk," Cas shot back. On any other day in this building, Cas would have looked away and said nothing. She would have just accepted that people never listened to someone like her and thought she was useless, because she knew that making waves might cause things to get worse. A lot worse. But there wasn't much worse than what was happening now.

"She's right."

Cas spun to face Diana, who smiled at her.

"There has to be something that we can use to create some kind of rope," Diana explained calmly. "And with all the broken wood around here, how hard could it be to make some kind of stretcher for Kaitlin that we can use to lower her to the ground?"

"Okay, then." Frankie clapped his hands together. "Spread out. Grab anything you think might be useful. No idea is too stupid to try."

"Thanks," Cas said. No doubt Z would have turned his anger on her had Diana not shot him down.

Diana shrugged. "I try to agree with people who aren't acting irrational." She glanced over toward Z, who was tucking a strand of hair behind Kaitlin's ear. He then leaned down and whispered something to the seemingly unconscious girl before he headed to the storage closet on the far side of the room. Frankie made for the cabinets. Tad stared at Frankie's back for several long seconds, looking as if he wanted to say something. Then, shaking his head, he walked over to ransack the teacher's desk.

"Why don't you sit while the rest of us search the room?" Diana offered Cas.

"Why?" Cas asked. "You don't think I'm capable of helping us get out of here?"

"Actually, I was thinking you look like you're going to pass out and that it might help us a whole lot more if you conserved your energy." Diana's eyes narrowed. Then she shrugged and turned away. "But if you want to be as stubborn as Z, go right ahead."

Humiliation burned Cas's throat and made her want to crawl under the table. Finally, she just blurted out, "I really am sorry. I just hate this school. Even before today, I've hated it."

Diana cocked her head to the side and frowned. "Then why are you here?"

"What do you mean?" Cas stiffened as Frankie yelled that he'd found a radio.

Cas took a step toward Frankie, but Diana stepped into her path. When Cas tried to go around her, Diana put a hand out to stop her.

"What?" Cas asked as the sound of static from the radio

filled the air. "Don't you want to hear what's happening out there?"

"It might also be helpful to figure out what's happening in here."

"What does that mean?" Cas pulled her bag up onto her shoulder and held it tight.

"You tell me. School doesn't start until next week." Diana looked hard at Cas. "You said you didn't have to be here and that you hate this place. So I was wondering why you came to school today."

Cas racked her brain for what to say. A second passed. Two.

Sweat snaked down her chest while Diana looked at her as if she already knew why Cas was here. A voice floated through the static.

On the other side of the room, guys fought over the dials as Cas thought about a lie to tell. Like the lies she told her father and her mother and the shrink every time they asked how she was feeling. But today was the day she'd decided to stop lying. She found herself looking at the girl she knew was the kind of daughter her own parents actually wanted, and when Diana asked again, "Why did you come here today, Cas? You must have had a reason," the truth just tumbled out.

"I came here to die."

1:00 P.M.

DIANA

− CHAPTER 37 −

DIANA STARED AT THE GIRL standing with her turquoise bag pulled against her, her chin raised as if waiting for Diana to act horrified that she'd ever consider what she had just admitted to.

"Quiet!" Frankie yelled as the static cleared. A nasal female voice filled the room.

". . . uncertain as to the location of the bomber, and after the last explosion, which we are told was detonated remotely, there is debate about how to proceed with the rescue mission. From what we have learned, the person behind the bombing is in communication with the police, and they are working hard to identify both the individual or individuals behind the attack and the location of any other explosive devices. Firefighters continue to fight the blaze from a distance while the three first responders caught in the last blast are being rushed to the hospital—"

Three firefighters could die or were already dead.

"God, this blows!" Z shoved one of the chemistry tables toward the wall.

"Shut up," Tad snapped. He leaned toward the radio, and Z caught his arm and jerked him back.

"Don't you tell me to shut up. You think you can—"

"How about you both shut up so the rest of us can listen?" Frankie said, getting in between the two guys and pushing them apart. "Some of us would like to know if we're going to live or die."

"Frankie's right," said Cas, still clutching her bag against her side. "We have problems enough without fighting among ourselves."

"Or maybe you guys just want to go along with Miss Princess here, because that's what you always do." Z started at Diana. "And that's what you expect people to do, because your father is some big-shot senator with a lot of money, and that makes you important." Z crossed his arms over his chest. "You ain't jack to me, and in case you didn't notice, you're still stuck in here the way we all are, so you aren't all that."

". . . confirmed that his daughter, Diana Sanford, is trapped inside."

Z's jaw clenched, and Diana gave the guy a satisfied smile.

"FBI and Homeland Security believe this to be an act of domestic terrorism, since no international group has thus far taken credit, but they are investigating all leads and working with local authorities to determine if it is safe for first responders to enter the building or if the threat of additional explosive devices is still credible."

"Which means Kaitlin is screwed if I don't get her out of here," Z said. "Did anyone find anything yet that looks like it will help?" When no one immediately said yes, Z threw up his hands and stalked back to the storage locker.

It was only then that Diana realized there was one person not huddled around the radio or looking for something to help them get out of the building: Rashid. His eyes were fixed on Kaitlin, but Diana wasn't sure he was actually seeing the dying girl in front of him. His mind seemed to be on something else.

Diana looked at Cas, who hadn't moved while the woman on the radio interviewed someone about first-responder procedure and how difficult it was to navigate this kind of situation when firefighters had already been injured by one device and no one knew if there were more. A bomb robot had been brought in and was entering the building now, and everyone was waiting to see what would happen next. The first responders were battling the blaze from a distance, but the fire was still burning. The people on the radio made it sound a lot like a game of chess where any move was one play from checkmate.

Once again, Diana looked out the window to see what was happening. She wondered whether Tim was there with her father, trying to move the pieces on the board.

Seven people were trapped in this room. Odds were that there were still more people in other parts of the building.

Diana glanced at Kaitlin and had to wonder how many were like this girl whose eyes stared at the ceiling as she gasped for air. Most everyone should have been out of the building when the first bomb went off. But people had still died, and the three firefighters caught in the last blast might not live.

Diana walked closer to the window while a commercial for insurance played on the radio.

"How about we put anything we find that can be useful in the center of the room? Like our captain said earlier, nothing is too crazy to consider," Diana said, giving Frankie a sweet smile, even though his handsome face made her want to scream. "We can listen to the news while we're doing that. And maybe, since Cas isn't up to moving around a lot, she can make another sign with all of our names on it."

"Why?" Rashid's head snapped up.

"To let the firefighters know we relocated from the third floor down here with you. If they're given the go ahead to enter the building again, we want them to know where we are."

Without waiting for approval, Diana grabbed a poster off the wall, found a black marker in the teacher's desk, and handed it to Cas. Then she walked over to the middle of the room where Frankie had shoved back a few desks to clear a space on the floor for dumping anything useful they found. So far there were two short extension cords, a couple of rolls of burlap-looking twine, and some metal rulers.

"Not a lot to work with so far," she commented. Frankie glanced at her and shrugged.

He'd asked her out a bunch of times, and she'd dodged at first because she knew his reputation with girls. No one went out with Frankie Ochoa without putting out. Everyone knew that.

So when she finally decided she wanted to break free of her perfect mold, he was the ideal choice. Their first date was a movie. The movie sucked, but making out with Frankie more than made up for it. She'd actually looked forward to seeing him at her father's Fourth of July party. Only not long after he arrived, Frankie told her he was going to the bathroom, and he never came back. No explanation. No apology.

"Don't worry. We'll figure something out," Frankie said. "I'm not the giving-up type."

"Yes, you are," she said as Cas asked Z for Kaitlin's last name and for his real one.

"Alex Vega. And hers is O'Malley. Kaitlin O'Malley," Z said as Frankie turned away from Diana. As if who she was wasn't important enough to matter. Just as Diana's father had so often done with her.

Well, Diana thought, *they were wrong.* They were both very wrong.

Cas finished writing. Diana helped put tape on the back of the sign while trying to decide what her next move should be. She didn't like waiting around, hoping things would turn out the way she wanted. She needed to do something.

The poster ripped as Diana yanked it through the narrow opening and finally was able to slap it to the brick wall next to the window. She ran her hand over the front to get the thing to stick as best she could, then waved out the window at the people standing in the parking lot. The wind pulled at the paper, and Diana knew it wouldn't stay in place for very long, but it would be long enough for the cameras to record the names. Then when the wind blew the paper off the wall, reporters would capture that image, too. It would make for a poignant moment of television. They would show the image over and over again while they read the names of those who were trapped inside, begging for help. Tim always said the framing of her father's narrative was just as important as the message. It was why Diana always had to look perfectly all-American. A picture was worth a thousand words, because rarely did anyone bother to read the words that went with the picture. It was the picture that drove them to action.

"Why do you dislike Frankie?" Cas asked.

"What do you mean?" Diana kept her eyes directed out the window, but inside, she went still. "I like him fine. Everyone does."

"You sound annoyed whenever you talk to him, and you looked worried when he got near your backpack."

"Maybe you heard me being stressed when I talked to Frankie," Diana deflected. "Or maybe you're just upset because you told me something you wish you hadn't." Cas looked away, and Diana lowered her voice to ask, "You said you came to school to die. How did you plan on doing it? Do you have a gun with you?"

Once again, Cas pulled her own bag close against her side. It looked mostly empty, but clearly there was still something inside.

The fear in Cas's eyes was all the answer Diana needed.

Diana glanced over her shoulder out the window, then turned back. "I think they've seen the sign," she said loud enough to make sure everyone in the room could hear. Cas directed her attention toward the window, and Diana tried to decide what to do next.

Tim would have an idea. But as much as her father listened to advice, he was the one who made the tough calls. If her father could do it, she could too.

The rest of the group hurried toward the window to look as the radio news anchor reported that firefighters were still battling the blaze and explosive experts were using all methods open to them to get in and rescue those still trapped in the building—seven of whom were located on the second floor.

". . . Members of the senator's staff have suggested that the target of today's ongoing attack is Senator Sanford's daughter, Diana. While authorities will not confirm that speculation, Senator Sanford has been under attack from many who believe his Safety Through Education bill will usher in what has been called a new version of McCarthyism."

"Well," Diana said, "at least they know where we are now. My father says—"

"No one gives a damn what your father says!" Z spun to

face her. "From what that announcer is saying, it's because of your father that we're in this mess."

Diana stepped forward. "My father had nothing to do with this. He's working to make the country safer."

"I'd say if he's trying to make things safer, he's already failed."

"It's not like he made the bombs that blew up this place." Tad jumped into the fray.

"Which means what? That he isn't responsible?" Z ignored Tad and leaned toward Diana. "Politicians are never to blame, right? It's never their fault when people do the stuff they encourage because, hey, they didn't actually do it themselves. Your father is telling kids to judge each other, but he's trying to pretend it's all about safety. I'm sure he won't be responsible, either, when teachers get rid of students who don't behave exactly the way they want by reporting so-called dangerous behavior or when students start taking matters into their own hands and start hurting each other."

"My father isn't saying he wants anyone to get hurt."

"Of course he is." Z laughed. "Teachers already hate me because of my tattoos and my hair. Now they have a great way to dump me from their classroom. And how long will it be before kids get jumped just for being different or because they're having a bad day? After all, your father and his law said it was okay."

"That's not what—"

"Your father's law is supposed to be for?" Z cut her off. "Yeah, like no one's heard that before. How about Tad here? Wanna bet people already look at him sideways because he's black? How long do you think it will take for some idiot to report him based on that alone?"

She dug her nails into her palms.

"And what about Rashid?" Z took a step toward her. "He's Muslim. Don't you think someone is going to find that scary for no reason? Or Cas here. She looks defensive. Could be she's hiding something. Or maybe there's some other kid looking to take that quarterback spot. Wow. What do you know? Suddenly Frankie is a suspicious character and his whole life should be turned inside out. That sounds great, don't you think, everyone?"

"That's not what my father is saying," Diana snapped.

Z took another step closer. "No? Then maybe you aren't listening. The nicer the words sound, the worse it always is."

"My father wants to make the world safer."

"God bless America, where we turn everyone against each other to keep us safe. Screw trust and friendship." Z spun around and pointed at Tad and Cas and Frankie. "How safe would you really feel if you were surrounded by spies ready to jump on anything you say or do? I'd rather get blown to bits right now if—"

"Quiet!"

Diana and Z turned toward Rashid, who had jumped up

from his stool and put his ear near Kaitlin's mouth. After a second, he yelled, "She's stopped breathing. Help me!" Only he didn't wait for anyone before climbing up on the table and straddling Kaitlin. He put his hands on her chest and started pushing against her again and again and again.

Diana stepped back as Z tripped over a fallen chair and yelled, "What do we do?"

"Put your hand on her forehead and gently push it back," Rashid said, never stopping the pulsing burst of pressure on Kaitlin's chest. "We have to keep her airway open."

Z's hand shook as he touched Kaitlin's forehead. His face was almost white as Rashid told him to get her mouth open. Z was a jerk, but he cared about Kaitlin. So did Rashid, and he didn't know the girl.

Rashid nodded and kept pulsing on her chest in a quick, steady rhythm with an intense look of concentration as he performed CPR.

"Is she breathing?" Cas asked.

"I don't know." Rashid was pushing too rapidly for Diana to tell if it was working. "Should I take her pulse?"

"No," Rashid said as he continued CPR.

Sweat dripped from Rashid's face. Diana waited for him to give up. But he kept going.

The woman on the radio was interviewing someone who recited the names of the trapped students and the information they'd been able to get about each of them.

"How long have I been doing this?" Rashid demanded.

"What?" Frankie asked.

"How long since I started CPR?"

The compressions were slowing. Rashid was getting tired. Still, he kept fighting.

"A couple minutes," Tad said. "At least two. Maybe three or four."

"Okay." Rashid stopped the compressions and leaned down to put his fingers on her neck.

"Why are you stopping?" Z asked.

Rashid closed his eyes, tilted his head, and frowned as Diana placed a hand on Z's shoulder to keep him from shouting again. After a moment, Rashid took a deep breath and his eyes opened.

Looking up at Z, he said, "She's got a pulse. She's okay."

Diana stared at Kaitlin as Z took her hand and held it tight while telling her that he wasn't going to let her die. Diana was certain no one, not one person in her whole life, had ever cared about her—the real her, not the perfect girl who smiled but the one who screamed behind the smile—as much as Z cared about Kaitlin.

And she was sure no one ever would.

1:09 P.M.

TAD

— CHAPTER 38 —

HELPLESS, TAD WATCHED Rashid kneeling on the desk, looming above Kaitlin and breathing hard. Sweating. As if he'd been on the field, running wind sprints. But instead of dashing up and down a field, Rashid had saved a life.

He hadn't freaked out. He'd just taken charge and done what needed to be done.

The guy had saved a life after Tad had basically accused him of causing the bombing.

All because of a shaved beard and the 911 call Rashid lied about.

". . . communication with authorities has threatened additional explosions if demands aren't met. Meanwhile, police dogs and a bomb robot are currently sweeping the areas around the entrance points for explosive devices while firefighters continue to battle the blaze on the east and south sides of the school. Of the three firefighters caught in the fourth explosion, two are in critical but stable condition while the other—"

"Thanks." Z put a hand on Rashid's shoulder. "I owe you."

Rashid shook his head and tried to step away from Z, but Z held on to his shoulder as Rashid insisted, "You owe me nothing. I only did what anyone would do."

"I couldn't do what you did." Frankie stepped in between Rashid and Z. "You're a serious hero, man. Where did you learn to do that? Because it didn't look anything like what they do on TV."

"My father." Rashid reached for a bottle of water and poured a little on a paper towel. He wiped his face with it as he looked past Frankie to where Kaitlin was breathing—not strong, but breathing. "My father is a doctor."

"Well, that explains it." Frankie slapped Rashid on the arm and added, "It's good we have someone who knows what to do if something bad happens."

Tad rolled his eyes and laughed. Leave it to Frankie to make people laugh even when there was nothing to laugh about. The bad just kept getting worse. Frankie not talking to him. The explosions. The fire. Being trapped in here with everyone hoping they didn't die. And if it weren't for Rashid spotting the bomb in the locker and telling Tad to run in the other direction, Tad might not be around to experience the bad at all.

". . . seven students are known to be trapped on the second floor. Of those, one is the daughter of Senator Sanford, who was in his office working on gaining additional support for his Safety Through Education bill when he learned of today's events. The senator, his wife, and several of his staff members are currently holding vigil outside with members of the other families who have loved ones trapped inside the school."

Frankie walked toward Diana. "Do you think the senator will be able to light a fire under them and get people in here to save us?"

"He'll try to make people pay attention." Diana looked away, toward the corner of the room.

"Is that the best you can do?" Z asked. "Your father is going to try?"

"What do you want me to say?" Diana shot back. "Yes. If the FBI and police insist on keeping the firefighters back, he'll talk to reporters and put pressure on them that way. The media has power. They don't just report news. The issues they select to put on the air shape how people think. Perception is everything in this world. And now that the news stations have our names, they'll be flashing photographs of all of us and talking to our families to add the human element to the story. The media will make people care. And when people care, action is actually taken."

"Which is good," Frankie said.

Tad coughed and glanced down. Wisps of smoke were coming under the door. They all had to get out of here soon.

"Is it good for us, or for her father and his career?" Z asked. "He's the one who's talking to the cameras right now, acting all humane and probably telling everyone that if his law was passed, this kind of thing wouldn't happen. Pretty great deal for him. Don't you think, Princess? If you died, you'd probably guarantee his election to the White House."

"Screw you," Diana spat.

"Screw me? Why don't you —"

"Hey, everyone," Tad interrupted. "It's time to get a grip. Yes, this sucks, and I think we can all agree that Diana's father's law sucks too, but we need to focus. Until they let the firefighters come in, we're on our own. I don't know about you, but I'd rather not be in this place if another bomb goes off. So maybe we should try to figure out how to escape instead of pointing fingers and screaming at each other."

Although how they were going to do that with the things Tad was looking at was beyond him. There were several eight-foot extension cords like the one in his hands, along with a small stepladder, several sizes of PVC pipes, twine, some small rolls of wire, a box of Bunsen burners, another box with rags, and a whole lot of other long sticks, glass tubes, laminated posters, and various odds and ends.

"Tad's right," Rashid said quietly. "Kaitlin needs a doctor. We have to find a way to build a stretcher or something that can lower her to the ground."

"We could break apart one of these tables," Z said, getting down on his hands and knees and looking underneath one of the black high-top desks.

"That might work," Tad said, walking over to examine the

table with Z. The chemistry desks had withstood a bunch of explosions, and they were still standing. As far as Tad was concerned, they couldn't get much sturdier than that.

"Help me flip this over," Z said, scrambling to his feet. "If we can break off the legs, we can use the top as a stretcher."

Tad grabbed one end as Z grabbed the other and grunted as they tipped the thing over.

"The table won't work," Rashid said.

"Why the hell not?" Z glared at him. "A stretcher has to be sturdy, and this is as sturdy as it comes."

"It'll never get through the window." Rashid didn't raise his voice in response to Z's anger as he explained, "And even if it could get through with Kaitlin on it, we don't have ropes strong enough to lower it to the ground."

"He's right," Frankie said. He was standing next to Cas with his hand on her shoulder. "We'll just have to come up with another plan."

". . . looks like the blaze to the south of the building is coming under control . . ."

"We'll figure something out," Rashid told Z. "I promise."

Z went back to the center of the room to rummage through the stuff with Tad. Frankie and Cas joined them as Rashid hurried back toward Kaitlin. Sympathy stormed in his eyes as he felt for a pulse and tried to get her to drink.

They also needed rope, but at this point Tad didn't see how anything they'd found could be used to make a stretcher. The

PVC pipes were obviously the strongest material they had, but as Cas and Frankie tried to come up with a way to use them with other things like the wire or balsa wood, Z was quick to point out the flaws. There was no way to attach them that would hold Kaitlin's weight.

Frustrated, Tad walked over to stand next to Rashid. "There's not enough here we can use."

Rashid nodded. "If we think it's safe, we could try Mr. Lott's room. The Robotics Club stores all sorts of things in there."

"That might be a good idea." It was. Once again, Rashid was smart and helpful. It made Tad feel worse about everything that had happened earlier. "I'm really sorry about before." Tad shoved his hands in his pockets and looked over at Rashid. "I mean it," Tad continued. "I know I was off, and I should have asked you about the phone call instead of just making assumptions. I was scared and I was stupid, and I would totally understand if you don't forgive me. Hell, I don't know if *I'd* forgive me."

"I called my sister," Rashid said quietly.

"Huh?"

"The call I made." Rashid sighed. "I thought I was going to die, and I wanted to talk to my sister so she wouldn't make the same mistakes I have."

And Tad thought he couldn't have felt any worse about how he'd behaved.

Rashid frowned. "Is Diana right?" he asked softly. "Will they really show our pictures on television?"

Tad let out the breath he had been holding in. It wasn't forgiveness, but it was a start.

"Yeah." He wiped his forehead on his shoulder. "We're probably all over the Internet. When we get out of here, we'll be famous. They'll want to interview Diana because of her father, but everyone is going to want to talk to us, too." And they'd want to know why he was in the school in the first place instead of partying with the football team.

He looked over at Frankie. Tad wasn't sure what he would say if he was asked. It would serve Frankie right if he told the truth. Maybe—

"That means everyone will see my face," Rashid said, pulling Tad's attention back to him. "First they'll see all of the pictures, and then they'll see only me."

Wait. What? No. "They're going to show all of our pictures. They'll see all of us."

"No," Rashid snapped. "They won't." His eyes were hollow. Fear colored every word as he pointed toward the window. "You know they won't. You just said it yourself. You know what it feels like to be judged by what you look like and instead of who you are, and you still did it. Everyone out there will do it too."

Tad wanted to tell Rashid that it wouldn't go that way. That Tad had been stupid, and no one else would be. But there was no point in lying.

Bombs. Terrorism. Muslim. Three things that always seemed to go together.

"The entire world is going to see my picture, and they'll judge me just like you did. They'll judge my family."

Frankie pushed himself up off the floor. "But you're not the one who bombed this place."

"No. I'm not," Rashid said, looking out the window.

Tad searched for something to say . . . anything. But he had nothing. Just a dull ache.

"The governor has put out a statement asking everyone to pray for the safety of those inside the building as well as the first responders who are fighting the blaze, along with the three who were . . ."

Rashid looked back at them all and let out a bitter laugh.

"What?"

"Do you think the governor or anyone outside will pray for me to get out safely?" He lowered his gaze to meet Tad's eyes. "Not that it matters. This is my punishment for thinking that being like all of you was the answer."

"I don't understand."

Rashid shrugged. "It was easier when I was younger. At least it seemed like it was. People didn't automatically think I was Muslim until I had a beard. We're not supposed to cut it when it grows in; did you know that? My cousins were jealous this summer because the beard made me look older. But here, it only seems to make people think about how I am different. Even my friends."

"That's why you shaved your beard? To be like everyone

else?" Diana asked from her perch near the window in the far corner of the room.

"No." Rashid looked down at his hands. "I shaved it because I wanted people to see me. I did it here so my family wouldn't see what I was doing before I was done. The school was letting students take new identification photographs today, and I hoped . . ." Rashid shrugged and shook his head.

For a second, everything was silent. The radio was still crackling, but Tad heard nothing other than Rashid's words and the pain behind them.

Finally Tad spoke. "You thought if you looked like everyone else, people would stop calling you names or looking at you sideways?" He understood that. He should. His life was filled with moments that made him wish he were someone else.

White kids calling him Monkey Man or Afro Boy—even though he kept his hair short.

When he was little, having his friends tell him their parents called him Half-Breed. Then the cleverer ones shouting "Zebra!"

People telling him that he couldn't understand what it was really like to be black because his daddy was white. He didn't count as black. He certainly didn't count as white. And when he told his family he was gay, he realized that no matter how much they might try to understand him, he'd never be the same as they were. He'd always be the odd man out who had to work to fit in.

And then Frankie made him feel that who he was was okay, before snatching that away.

Tad's heart beat faster. His palms sweated even more as the memory of those moments twisted in his gut.

"Boo-freakin'-hoo," Z said, dropping a box of stuff onto the floor. Kaitlin jerked in her sleep, and Rashid moved to her side as Z said, "You shaved—something a zillion guys do every day —and your family is going to hate your makeover. Sorry, but I'm not sorry. At least you have a family to give a crap, so how about we stop telling sob stories and figure out how we're going to get Kaitlin to the paramedics and the rest of us out of this place?"

Z crossed the room to the storage closet. He disappeared inside, and Tad said, "I think most of us in this room can understand what you're dealing with."

Cas nodded.

"Do you think anyone would assume any of you could be a killer because of how you look or how you pray?" Rashid asked.

"No, but I've had people make assumptions about me because I'm black." Tad swallowed hard, looked at Frankie, and said, "And also because I'm gay." Now that he'd admitted it to someone outside his family, it was like a balloon inflated inside him, waiting to be popped.

"You're gay?" Diana asked from the corner.

He nodded, never taking his eyes off Frankie. "Yeah. News flash. Macho football players can be gay."

"How about we do true confessions later and worry about

escaping now?" Frankie said, grabbing a couple of extension cords off the ground. Tad had come to the school today to force Frankie to face him and admit the truth. To admit that they had been more than friends and to tape that admission. He hadn't planned on showing the tape to anyone. He just wanted proof that he hadn't fooled himself and to let Frankie know eventually that it existed. Then Frankie would finally understand what it was like to have someone twist you up inside and make you worry about who you were and whether there was something wrong with you. Tad had earned that. He'd earned having the upper hand for once.

And maybe he would have used it.

Tad swallowed hard at that thought. He told himself he'd never wanted to use the tape, but he'd been angry and tired and maybe he'd wanted to make the tape because he didn't want Frankie to get a pass the way he always did. The way Tad never could.

Knowing that he'd been angry enough to think that way sucked, but it didn't make it any less true. And if he wanted Frankie to face it all, now was the time. Frankie could deny they had kissed. He could deny all the late-night phone calls, but everyone in the room would still hear what Tad said.

The words sprang to Tad's lips, but as he looked around, he realized he didn't want to talk about Frankie and his choices. Frankie wasn't important.

So instead, Tad said, "If we think it's safe enough, Rashid said there might be some things we can use in Mr. Lott's room."

Rashid nodded. "I can go. I'm in Robotics Club. I know where everything is kept."

"What about the smoke?" Cas asked.

Rashid turned to her. "I can hold a piece of wet paper towel over my mouth. I won't be gone long."

"I'll go with you," Tad offered.

"You don't trust me to go on my own?"

"Of course I trust you," he shot back. "But I was in that room during the first explosion, and I know where the floor is cracked. I can help."

He waited to see if Rashid turned him down.

He didn't. "Wet a paper towel for each of us." Tad reached for the water bottle next to Kaitlin as Rashid added, "You guys should close the door behind us to keep the smoke out until we come back."

"Ready?" Tad asked, handing one of the wet paper towels to Rashid.

"As ready as I'm going to be," Rashid answered, wrapping the edge of his shirt around the handle on the door, turning it, and pushing it open. "Let's go."

They stumbled through the smoke and debris of the hallway to Mr. Lott's classroom. Despite breathing through the paper towel, Tad tasted char and smoke. Mr. Rizzo still lay on the floor. Unmoving. Tad pressed the wet paper towel tighter to his mouth to keep from throwing up as he stepped over the body and slipped into the room.

"Who was the friend you were going to meet today?" Rashid

questioned as he hurried toward the boxes in the corner of the room.

"Does it matter?" Tad asked.

Rashid looked at him for several long seconds through the haze of dark gray smoke. Finally he said, "No, it doesn't. Not to me."

1:18 P.M.

FRANKIE

— CHAPTER 39 —

FRANKIE LET OUT a breath of relief the minute Tad and Rashid went out the door. He'd dodged the bullet this time. Hearing Tad's voice when he was coming down from the third floor had unsettled him, but when he got through the doorway and saw him in those clothes . . . Tad had changed clothes to meet with him. And he was pretty sure he knew why.

During one of their midnight calls, they both had the same movie on at their houses. It was some movie about a geeky girl and a popular guy, and the girl changed her look in order to get the guy's attention. Tad turned the movie off and said people should just accept each other for who they were. Frankie had laughed and said something like sometimes the only way people took something seriously is if you forced them to.

Clearly Tad wanted to be taken seriously, and if they got out of here, Frankie would have to come up with something to tell him to make him back off.

He liked Tad. He did, but he couldn't be what Tad wanted.

The conversations they had were great. They had a lot in common. It was no wonder they clicked.

It was just one kiss.

He should never have done it. He stepped over a line that no one in his family or his friends would ever understand. Even he didn't get why he'd crossed that line. He wasn't interested in guys. That wasn't who he was supposed to be. He was supposed to date girls like Diana. If he hadn't bailed on her, he would never have seen Tad on the Fourth of July. This was Tad's problem. Not his.

He shook his head and held up the two rolls of twine he'd found in one of the drawers. "I know this stuff isn't strong enough on its own, but we might be able to make it work if we braid it together into something stronger. What do you think, Diana?"

She glanced over at him and blinked. "What?"

"What do you think about using the twine to create a stronger rope?"

"Why are you asking her?" Z laughed. "Does she look like the Girl Scout type?"

"No, but I'm betting by her bracelet that she knows how to braid things," Frankie said. Diana looked down at her wrist as if surprised that he'd noticed the bracelet. "Am I right?"

"You can't really expect us to go out that window on a rope made of braided twine like we're deranged superheroes." Cas looked up at him. Her face was sweaty and streaked with dirt and under it all her skin looked pasty. But her voice was sharp when she said, "There's no way I can do that."

"You survived a bunch of explosions, a fire, and climbing down through a collapsed floor." He looked her dead in the eyes, the way he did to his receiver as he was calling a Hail Mary play when the team was losing. "I'm thinking you can do just about anything if you want to."

"I'm guessing she doesn't want to," Diana said, crossing to the middle of the room. "But I do. I didn't come to this school today to die."

"I don't think any of us came here thinking we'd end up dead," Frankie said.

"Are you sure about that?" Diana glanced down at Cas, who looked down at the floor.

"What are you—"

The door burst open, and a coughing Rashid and Tad hurried inside through a cloud of smoke. Tad dumped the stuff he was carrying on the ground, turned, and slammed the door behind him. Kaitlin whimpered as Rashid shoved a bunch of the paper towels back under the door.

"Did you find any rope?" Z demanded.

"Sorry, man." Tad turned from the door. "No rope."

Damn.

"But we found something we think we can turn into a stretcher. There was a canopy someone must have—"

"Without rope, what's the point?" Z ran a hand through his

hair. "We don't have time to wait around for Princess here to braid a bunch of twine together that we don't know will be long enough or strong enough or . . ." He looked around, then up at the ceiling. "What about the wires in the ceiling? It's not like they're being used for electricity right now."

"I tried pulling out electrical wires earlier," Tad said. "They're strong enough to hold just about anything, but impossible to yank out of the ceiling or the walls. Trust me, I tried."

Z glared at him. "And I'm supposed to give up because 'you tried'?"

"Tad has some muscle," Frankie added.

"And of course you'd know," Z shot back, climbing up on one of the high-top desks. "Do you think I'm going to put Kaitlin's life in the hands of two people who are stupid enough to spend their time jumping other guys?"

"What the hell does that mean?" Frankie clenched a fist as his heart pounded hard. "I don't jump other guys."

"So you just let them tackle you?" Z looked from Frankie to Tad, then back at Frankie, and smiled. "Maybe that's exactly what you do. Tad here just told us he's gay. How about you, Captain of the Football Team? Have you been feeling up Tad's muscles? That how you know how strong he is?"

"Up yours."

"You're going to make the team jealous if they hear you say that."

"Stop it!" Diana shouted. "This is stupid. Frankie isn't gay."

"You calling me stupid, Princess?" Z shoved the table in front of him as blood pounded hard in Frankie's ears. "Maybe you should look in the mirror."

"Screw you!" Diana shouted.

"Don't let him get to you," Tad said. "He's just trying to get under your skin."

"Yeah," Frankie agreed. "He's not worth listening to or getting upset over. He just wants to make everyone else as miserable as he is."

"You think you know me?" Z pressed his hands against the ceiling tile next to the light and shoved it upward. "None of you know anything about me. So don't pretend you do."

"And you don't know anything about me or Frankie or anyone else in this room," Diana said. "We're all stuck and we're all scared, and just because—"

"Scared?" Z looked down from above at her. "Are you scared, Princess? Scared that for the first time in your life, you have to actually look out for yourself because there isn't someone around to do it for you?"

"How about you stop taking your crap out on us." Frankie shoved the table Z was standing on. Z put his hands on the ceiling to keep from falling as Frankie shouted, "Just because you're pissed and scared doesn't mean we have to be your personal punching bags. If you hadn't noticed, we haven't done anything to you."

"Yeah." Z looked down at all of them from above, sweat

dripping down his forehead as he nodded. "None of you have ever done a damn thing. And if we get out of here, you can keep on doing nothing. "

Z yanked the light fixture downward. Dust and bits of tile rained from the ceiling as the light now hung an inch or two below it. Z continued to pull at it and budged it just a couple of inches more.

Frankie and Tad had both been right about the wire being strong.

"Now, that's impressive," Diana said. "At this rate, you'll have enough wire to make a ladder by Christmas. We're saved."

"Shut up," Z said. "At least I'm trying to get the hell out of here instead of waiting around, hoping for the best."

Z pulled on the light again and snapped the plastic of the fixture while the wires barely moved.

"Z's right," Frankie said as Diana glared at him. "We have to keep trying. Why don't you start braiding together some of the twine, and Rashid and Tad can build whatever stretcher they were thinking about while Z and I work on getting the wires out of the ceiling?"

If nothing else, it was something to do besides talk.

"I don't need your help," Z said. "I don't need anyone's goddamn help."

"You needed my help when we had to get Kaitlin out from under that air conditioner," Frankie said quietly. "I'd like to help get her to a doctor. Okay?"

"... authorities are pursuing leads on the identity of those believed to be behind setting the bombs. Meanwhile, the bomb units have disarmed a bomb discovered in the field house, and they are continuing to search for other devices as firefighters battle the fire, which finally appears to be under control. Two girls who escaped out of a window on the east side of the building are being treated for cuts and second-degree burns, and we are sorry to report that one of the firefighters injured by the device detonated when first responders went into the building has died from—"

"Yeah." Z nodded and looked down at Frankie. "Sure. Feel free to help me tear the hell out of this school. You seem to like it fine, but it never did anything for me."

Frankie climbed up onto the table and wrapped one of the wires around his hand, then pulled as hard as he could. *Damn.* The wire barely moved.

"Here, Diana, we also found a couple more small extension cords," Rashid said behind him. "If you braid the cords with the twine and any wire Z and Frankie get, it might be strong enough to lower Kaitlin down after we finish with the stretcher."

"Looks like we have to break this place apart faster if we're going to help with Rashid's plan," Frankie said as Z yanked down on the light fixture and sent it crashing to the table, pulling several feet of wire with it.

"I . . ." Z tugged the wires. "Hate . . ." Z pulled again. "This . . . school." He leaned his whole weight into it and almost crashed to the floor as more wire came free.

Frankie wiped his forehead with the back of his hand "Wow, you really do hate this school. Guess that's why you aren't ever here. If your parents decide to crack down, let me know. I could use another offensive tackle to protect me."

Z wiped his palms against his shorts. "Well, my father died in a car accident when I was two, so I'm thinking he's not going to be cracking down on my studies anytime soon. My mom was pretty good at keeping me in line, but the last couple of years, she didn't have a lot of time to dedicate to it."

"Why not?"

"Well." Z panted. "It's kind of hard to focus on driving your son to school and watching him do his homework when you're strapped to a hospital bed, busy trying to keep cancer from killing you." He looked at Frankie and shrugged. "Guess you didn't expect that, did you?"

No. No, he didn't.

He tried to come up with something to say, but words failed him as he stood on the chemistry desk, looking at the guy who everyone knew liked to cut class and cause trouble.

"Did your mother's treatment work?" Rashid quietly asked from the middle of the room.

Z glanced toward Rashid, who was kneeling next to a grid of metal strips he was fastening together with wire and twine. Z's hands squeezed the wires he was holding so hard that Frankie was amazed they didn't cut into his flesh. And he felt the answer to Rashid's question before Z said just as quietly, "She trusted the doctors, who said they were going to beat the cancer. She trusted me when I said I would never let anything happen to her. She died three weeks ago."

"Man, I'm sorry," Frankie said, thinking about his own parents. They told him how to act and why and what kind of person he should be. He hated how they got angry whenever he questioned going to youth group or tried to take a class they thought was pointless. They wanted their son to be the best— the most successful. But as much as he hated what they wanted for him and expected from him and how he had to push things he might want to the side . . . "I can't imagine—"

"No, you can't." Z hopped desks, grabbed another fluorescent light, and screamed as he yanked down on it.

The voice on the radio faded, then came back up to full, static-filled volume as Z threw his weight into taking down the light.

Ceiling tiles around the light area cracked. Dust and splinters fell from above as something gave in the ceiling. Cas screamed, and Frankie rushed forward as Z fell flat on his back onto the chemistry table.

"Are you okay?" Frankie asked as Cas and Tad appeared on either side of him.

Z looked up at the colorful wires snaking down from the ceiling and coughed. "You're right, Tad. The wire is really strong." He coughed again, and Frankie put his hand on Z's back as Z struggled to sit up. When he was seated on the table, he looked up at the ceiling and asked, "How much more of it do you guys need?"

Rashid looked down at the braiding Diana was working on and the stretcher he and Tad were creating and smiled. "How much more can you get?"

"I guess we'll find out." Frankie grinned back. "But it might help if someone found something we can cut these with."

"Let me do that," Cas said as Rashid started to get up. "I want to do something to help."

She winced and swayed once she was on her feet. Even if they built the strongest rope ladder in history, Frankie wasn't sure how she'd be able to use it when she was weak and had only one usable arm.

As Z grabbed a fistful of wires and tugged them another foot or so out of the ceiling, Frankie stepped toward the window to see what was happening. The radio was cutting in and out while the announcer gave the weather report and said they would be talking to an FBI spokesman in a few minutes.

It was hard to tell what was going on outside. There were ambulances and fire trucks and people in uniforms and with FBI jackets huddled together.

"Do you think there really are more bombs ready to go off?"

"They must think that there are, or the firefighters would be here rescuing us by now," Diana said.

"I don't get it." Tad frowned. "I mean, if you're pissed off enough to blow up a school, why not just blow it up all at once? Why do it piece by piece?"

"It's dramatic," Frankie admitted.

"It sucks," Z snapped.

"Frankie's right. And I'm betting the bomber is waiting for another rescue attempt before setting off any remaining charges," Diana said. "Killing a whole bunch of people at the very end of whatever this is would make a pretty strong statement."

"Killing more people would make a statement?" Cas stared at Diana. "That makes no sense. None of this makes any sense."

"The higher the body count, the bigger the story. And the more they'll talk about the person who caused the tragedy and the reason behind it, instead of the people who died in the tragedy itself," Diana said. "Haven't you ever noticed that one person getting shot gets covered for an hour or maybe a day, but if there are lots of people killed at once, the media runs stories for weeks? The killers' pictures are plastered on the news day and night, and experts talk about who they are and analyze why they did what they did. And if the killers get away with it, the story becomes even bigger. Congress and the Senate hold hearings. Anyone who plans something like this has to do it in a big way, or it gets forgotten."

"And if the victims are rich and white and their fathers are important, the story is even bigger," Tad added. "Right, Diana?"

"I didn't create this system," she said stiffly. "The only way a person can make a real difference is to know the rules of the game and use them to win."

"I respect that," Frankie said. It was one of the things he

and Diana were in step on. The desire to reach the goal, even if it made no sense to anyone else. Winning came in a lot of forms, depending on a person's perspective. And when you were a winner, you had to recognize when something was a losing move and change course before it took you out of the game.

Cas crossed the room and handed a pair of scissors to Z. Rashid put his head down and got back to work on the stretcher. The radio crackled.

"If we're lucky, it'll start raining any minute," Frankie said, breaking the silence. "That could put out the remaining fires and screw up any other bombs so they won't go off."

"Hands up of anyone here who actually feels lucky." Z looked slowly at each one of them. "Because my luck is pure crap, and Kaitlin has—" His eyes softened. "Well, she had the bad luck of insisting on being my friend when I told her I didn't need one. She tried to save me from myself, and now she's the one who needs saving because she was sure she could talk me out of making another bad choice. Yeah, no luck on my end. How about you guys?"

Tad looked at Frankie and kept his hands at his side. Diana looked toward the back corner of the room.

Frankie shrugged and raised his hand. Then he smiled. "A building exploded, and I'm not dead. I'd rate that as lucky. How about you, Rashid?"

Rashid looked away from Kaitlin and put his arm up with a nod. "Living with my family's disappointment is better than not being alive at all."

Frankie looked over at Cas, who had taken a seat on one of the stools and was looking down at the ground. "Cas? Feeling lucky to be alive?"

Cas lifted her eyes and shook her head. "Actually, no. Everything would be easier if I was dead."

1:34 P.M.

CAS

— CHAPTER 40 —

"You don't mean that," Frankie said, staring at her. Just over an hour ago, Cas would never have dreamed that Frankie Ochoa would look at her with such intense concern. Only he was wrong, because she meant every word. She still remembered the way the gun felt in her hands.

The metal had been cool. The weight almost comforting in the promise that the gun could do what nothing else had been able to. Make it all go away.

She wanted to look away, but instead she forced herself to meet Frankie's eyes. "I shouldn't. I know I should feel lucky to be alive, but as much as I want to, I don't. Not entirely."

"Yeah," Z said quietly. "Me too. It's hard to feel lucky to be alive when you still might die and you're not sure if living is any better." Z looked over at the girl who hadn't opened her eyes in far too long. Kaitlin was quiet. Still. "If it weren't for Kaitlin, I might have run toward the explosion. And even then, I still thought about it."

"So you're a coward." Diana looked at him as if daring him

to fight. When he didn't, she added, "Killing yourself is taking the easy way out. That's what cowards do."

"Anything that permanent seems like a pretty hard choice to me," Frankie said. "That's probably why I've never considered doing it."

Of course he didn't understand. He was talented and popular—exactly what Cas's father wished she could be.

"Never?" Z turned to Frankie. "Not once?"

"No. Of course not." Frankie crossed his arms over his chest. "I don't like feeling depressed. I work my way out of it."

"Depression isn't like root beer. It's not as if you either like it or you don't." Z shook his head. "Sometimes you feel the world caving in piece by piece, and there doesn't seem to be anyone who gives a damn that you're slowly being crushed. You're telling me your life is so perfect that you've never felt that way?"

Falling apart, piece by little piece. Yes. That was exactly how she felt. Each day another pebble chipped off—almost too insignificant to notice, until one day the rest of the rock broke away because there was nothing underneath to help it stand.

"There's always someone around or another choice you can make," Frankie said.

"No, there isn't."

Frankie turned back toward her.

"Sure, you can always turn to someone." She swallowed hard and shook her head, wishing she hadn't said anything but knowing she couldn't stop now. "But that doesn't always mean they can help. It's hard for someone to help when they think the person standing in front of them is weak and broken and needs to have their life taken over."

"Anyone who is thinking about committing suicide is weak, and when you tell someone you are thinking about killing yourself, you most certainly are broken," Diana said.

"Most really broken people don't know they are broken," Rashid said.

Cas turned to look at the guy who had been working quietly on the floor. He was so unassuming, it was easy to forget he was there. The guy was a real hero. He'd saved Kaitlin's life and was helping to get them out of there. By any definition, Rashid was a leader. He should be the center of attention. And yet Cas thought of Frankie as the leader, and maybe even Z, because of how they pushed themselves forward.

Rashid met Cas's eyes with a steady gaze, "Those who are the most damaged don't ever admit they need help. It takes strength to admit that you want something to change, and it takes even more courage and strength to try to change it."

"But what if you've tried to change things and nothing is different?" Cas wrapped her good arm around herself.

"Then you try something else. Isn't that why we're all in this room together right now?" Rashid said. "We could have stayed where we were when the bombs went off and given up. Instead we're still working to get out. We're building a stretcher that we don't know will work and making ropes that could give way beneath us. But we're doing it anyway because fighting to live is hard. It's supposed to be. Giving up is the easy part."

"How do you know?" The hollowness inside Cas threated to overwhelm her. "Have you ever woken up in the morning and the idea of getting out of bed made you want to scream and never stop screaming? Have you ever had your parents pretend to reward you by taking you shopping for clothes they think will make you more popular because to them that's going to make it all better, or had your father take you to a shrink who tells you that you want to be unhappy and that you are imagining all of your problems?"

"Maybe your shrink is right," Diana said. "Could it be you're making problems bigger than they are because you want people to pay attention to you. Sometimes the only way to get people to pay attention is to force them to —"

"You think I'm making problems bigger than they are?" Cas pressed a shaky hand to her stomach. "Maybe I wanted attention so bad that I let one girl slam me into a locker and then push me to the ground. Maybe I even wanted two of her friends to hold me down while she kicked me in the chest and the stomach and told the others to help her. Maybe it's my fault I can't remember what happened after that because she kicked me so hard, I hit the back of my head against the floor and blacked out."

Cas remembered waking up in fear. Fear of the sadness in her mother's eyes as she told Cas she was going to be okay and fear of the way her father screamed at anyone who would listen about how he wouldn't take what happened to his daughter lying down. He wanted people arrested. He was going to sue, because his daughter was going to be scarred for life. People were going to pay.

Frankie walked over to her. He put his arm around her shoulder, and tears sprang to her eyes. "You lost a lot of blood, Cas," Frankie said quietly to her. "You should sit down and rest."

"I don't want to sit down." Cas shook off his arm. She didn't want to be pathetic. She didn't want to be the one who was so weak that people naturally assumed she needed their protection. "I'm tired of people telling me to take it easy or to let things go because I'm just creating drama to get attention." She looked at Diana, standing not far from the window. Cas swiped at a tear and swallowed down the others burning her throat and asked, "Was it okay for a girl and her friends to hate me because I wasn't part of their crowd and I didn't dress like them? Or how about you tell me exactly how it was my fault that the most popular girl in school decided that I was the person anonymously posting pictures of her boyfriend and suggesting he should break up with her?"

Diana never looked away, and she didn't speak. She just stood there — still as a stone, like everyone else in the room. Cas stood just as still, even though everything inside was racing.

For a second, the only sounds in the room were the muted shouting coming from the rescue workers outside, the chopping sound of a helicopter, and the siding-company commercial playing on the radio station.

"You were bullied." Tad finally broke the silence.

"Bullied." Bitter laughter bubbled through the tears. "God, I hate that word."

". . . path through the field house after a fifth device was uncovered and disarmed and removed. Officials . . . believe there is . . . another device, which is why they are . . . additional precautions to ensure . . . as . . . fire . . ."

Tad clicked off the radio. "The batteries are dying. We can turn it back on in a few minutes, once we're ready to try out the stretcher and the ropes."

Because then they'd need to know if it was necessary to risk their lives on a two-story drop. If there was another bomb in the building, Cas knew the answer would be yes. And then what would happen to her?

"Why don't you like the word?" Frankie asked quietly.

"Why?" Cas blinked and looked at the guy who had helped her get this far. A high school god—someone who would never understand what it was like to look in the mirror and wish that you were completely different. *"Bullied* is too easy a word. My father uses that word all the time. So does my shrink."

"I still don't get what the problem is," Frankie said. "It's just a word."

Cas winced as she shifted her injured arm and was glad for the pain, because it was better to focus on that than on the ache growing in her heart. "Have you ever been bullied?"

It was a dumb question, because he was the football captain. He was popular. If anything, he was probably the one who did the bullying.

But he surprised her by saying, "Yeah."

"How?"

"How?"

"How were you bullied?" she asked. "What happened to you?"

Frankie shoved his hands in the pockets of his shorts and shrugged. "Usual sports stuff. Someone put mayonnaise in my helmet and spray starch in my jockstrap. That kind of thing."

"How about you?" Cas asked, turning toward Tad. "Have you been bullied?"

"I've had guys bigger than me shove me in the halls and say stupid crap online to me. It's the way things go. Everyone goes through it."

"Has everyone been beaten up while other kids videoed what was happening and posted it online instead of going to get help?" Sweat trickled down her cheek. The memory played over and over in her head. "Has everyone had to change schools because once you went back, the same people who broke your ribs were threatening to do the same thing to anyone who was your friend so any friends you had suddenly found new places in the lunchroom to sit and new people to walk home with? Have you been beaten so badly you felt like you were going to die, only to realize how much easier life would have been if you had?"

She held her breath. Her heart pounded harder with every

second that passed as she stood there—waiting. For Frankie . . . for Tad or Rashid or Diana or Z to say something.

Sympathy.

Outrage.

Comfort.

Something.

The sound of a helicopter came closer and then faded.

A siren sounded outside, then went silent.

Someone on a bullhorn shouted something that was impossible to understand.

And no one inside the room said a word as Cas waited, understanding their discomfort and hating them for it at the same time.

When it was clear that no one was going to speak, she nodded. "That's what I thought."

"You're right," Rashid said. "*Bullying* is an easy word, and I feel like I should say something to make it better. But I don't know what."

"Neither do I," Tad said.

Cas blinked. Tears welled up, and she shook her head to ward them off. "It doesn't matter."

"If it didn't matter, you wouldn't have tried to kill yourself," Z said. "Unless you were just saying that to get attention."

"Leave her alone." Frankie stepped closer to Cas.

"She doesn't want to be left alone." Z barked a bitter laugh. "If she did, she'd be standing in the corner like Diana over there, pretending none of us exist, instead of letting you all know that for a lot of people, life isn't about football games and parties and making out in your basement, hoping your parents don't come down and catch you. Life sucks, and there aren't any words anyone can ever say that will make that better for me or Cas or the majority of people who don't have parents who think their crap smells like roses." Z pushed the desk next to him and strode to the window. "This all sucks." He hung out the window and yelled, "Do you hear me? If you're going to blow this place up, go ahead and do it now, because we're never getting out!"

"You don't mean that," Rashid said, looking over at Kaitlin, who trembled in her sleep. At least Cas wanted to think she was sleeping. Kaitlin could be in a coma at this point. How would any of them know?

"Don't I?" Z looked over his shoulder. "Life is crap, and no one in this building ever gave one damn what was happening in my life until my mother was dead. Who cares about the guy who looks like a screwup and cuts summer school because his mother might die any day and he didn't want her to die alone? Nah. Just send the mother who the school was told died a letter telling her that her son is going to have to repeat junior year because he didn't finish precalc. Is it any wonder I came to this place to let Mr. Casey know how much I appreciated his concern for my well-being? Kaitlin thought if I just talked to him, he'd understand how bad things were, but I know words don't do squat."

"He's right," Cas said, stepping toward Z. "Words don't make anything better. They're just the first step, and most people don't bother to follow through with the others. Words are easy."

"Yes." Tad nodded. He pushed up the sleeves of his dirty tux shirt, looked at Frankie, and said, "Yeah. They are."

1:47 P.M.

Z

— CHAPTER 41 —

KAITLIN GASPED FOR AIR. Rashid was up and next to her before Z moved to her other side. He held his breath as he watched Rashid check Kaitlin's pulse before shaking his head.

"What?" Z asked. "What's going on?"

Kaitlin moaned. Her eyes fluttered, and Z took her hand as he looked desperately at Rashid. Kaitlin's fingers were ice-cold.

"I don't know." Rashid took her pulse again. "She's still breathing, but it's getting shallower and her pulse is weaker than it was before. I don't know what to do."

"Can you do CPR again?" Z asked. "It worked before."

"Not unless she stops breathing." Rashid had given the answer Z knew was coming. He'd spent too much time in hospitals not to. "The swelling in her legs is worse. There's probably internal bleeding. I just don't know what more any of us can do."

Z gripped Kaitlin's hand and closed his eyes.

He had done this to her. If he'd answered her message today, she wouldn't have come looking for him. She would be healthy and whole if it weren't for him.

"If we get her to a doctor, there still might be a chance," Rashid said. A hand touched Z's shoulder, and he opened his eyes to see Rashid's looking at him. "The stretcher is almost done. It's not very strong, but Kaitlin is light, and if we strap her to it with the electrical wire . . ."

"I can try to braid the twine and the cords together faster," Diana said, and Tad added, "I'll help. Rashid can finish getting the stretcher ready, and I can work with Diana. We'll get her out of here, Z."

Would they?

"I can't just stand here and do nothing." Z paced toward the window. "There was nothing I could do for my mom. Nothing at all. But it seems like the fire is under control, and the radio said the firefighters were coming in soon. Maybe I can help them by moving stuff on this side so they can get through." He turned and headed back to Kaitlin.

"I can help," Frankie said.

"No," he snapped, and looked at Kaitlin's face, wishing she'd open her eyes. But it was like his mother all over again. Shallow breathing. Eyes closed.

"Look," Frankie said, "I can go one way and you can go the other. Two of us can check out all the stairwells faster that way while the others work on the rope. If one of us hears firefighters or spots a path that can be cleared, we can let the other know."

Z's knee-jerk refusal died on his lips. "Fine."

Frankie clapped his hands together. "Let's do it." Frankie headed for the door and Z turned to Rashid. "Take care of her for me. She's special."

Rashid nodded. "I will, Z."

Z looked at the terrifyingly slight, almost imperceptible, rise and fall of Kaitlin's chest. "She'd want you to call me Alex."

"Okay. Alex," Rashid said. "But when we get out of here, you'll have to tell me why you're called Z."

"I will," Z promised. Frankie opened the door. Smoke and dust came through as Frankie disappeared down the hall.

As Z was leaving, he whispered to Cas, "I meant what I said before. I get wanting to die."

Before she could say anything, Z ran.

When truth is buried underground, it grows, it chokes, it gathers such an explosive force that on the day it bursts out, it blows up everything with it.

—Émile Zola

1:51 P.M.

RASHID

— CHAPTER 42 —

SOMETHING WENT *SNAP* in the hall—probably Z or Frankie had stepped on a tile. Then things got quiet.

No one moved.

"What did Z say to you?" Diana glanced over at Cas.

"Nothing." Cas looked out the doorway and shook her head. "It's not important. What's important is getting out of here."

Rashid took a deep breath and nodded. "You're right. Since they can't get a ladder up here and Kaitlin might not have time to wait for Frankie and Z to come up with another option, we should keep working on the stretcher until we hear otherwise."

Tad frowned at the door before nodding. "We're almost there. The metal strips seem secure. They might hold together as long as the rope doesn't give way. Diana, what do you think?"

"I think you should worry about your part and I'll worry about mine."

"Don't fight," Cas said from the doorway that Frankie and Z had just disappeared through. Rashid saw the tears that glistened in her eyes as she asked, "Can we turn the radio back on? Maybe they'll tell us help is finally coming."

Rashid clicked on the radio before heading over to help Tad. There was the buzz of static, then the announcer telling everyone that the firefighters were making progress. The fire was contained to the west side, and they hoped to have it out soon.

"With one person of interest being questioned, authorities are now working to find another individual they have confirmed is involved in this terrible bombing. A source confirms that the individual is one of the students trapped on the second floor of the school. With four bombs having already gone off, there appears to be one explosive device still inside the school that could detonate at any time."

Another bomb was ready to go off, and the bomber was one of *them.*

They all looked at Rashid.

Of course they would look at him. Everyone outside was probably also assuming he was the bomber after that report. A Muslim with a family from Palestine. Of course he must be radicalized. Angry. Eager to strike. He didn't care what they thought out there. Maybe he had when this started, but not now. The only people whose opinions mattered were the ones inside this room. "I am not part of this."

He looked over at Kaitlin.

Rashid hadn't wanted to say it aloud, but he was almost sure she wouldn't make it. He wasn't his father, but he'd learned enough from him to know the odds were bad when he first saw her and were getting worse with each minute that passed. If they thought he had caused this . . . that he had gone against everything he had ever been taught . . .

"I didn't do this."

"Of course not." Tad stood up and stepped over the cords and the stretcher and everything else in the middle of the floor. "It's not you, and it sure as heck isn't me."

"How do we know that?" Cas asked. "You could be lying. Anyone in this room could be lying, and we wouldn't know until it was too late."

"I don't believe he's lying." Rashid stepped around the desk to stand at Tad's side. He'd seen Tad's face when he realized there was a bomb in the locker. He hadn't a clue what he was looking at until it was almost too late.

"You can't know that for sure," Diana said. She'd crossed to the door and peered down the hall.

"He had a chance to get out of the school after the bombing, and he didn't take it," Rashid said, then turned toward Cas. "Tad rescued me instead and got trapped with the rest of us."

"That proves nothing," Cas shot back. "He might be a suicide bomber. He might want to die to prove his point."

"Dying doesn't prove a point." Rashid threw up his hands and kicked a box of Bunsen burners across the floor. "It's crazy that some people think suicide bombing is a noble thing that will change the world. All it does is kill people. Killing doesn't change minds. It doesn't change the Koran or the teaching of Allah that taught me to be kind to all people and humble in all things. It just kills."

"And trust me when I say that I don't want to die," Tad added.

"But they think one of us was working with the other bomber," Cas said.

Another bomb, Rashid thought. "If they are right and there is another bomb, the bomber would want to make sure it went off."

They all turned toward the door.

"Z came up with the plan to leave," Tad said. "What if he was just trying to get away so he could detonate the last bomb?"

"What did Z say to you?" Diana stormed toward Cas. "When he left, what did he say?"

Cas looked toward Tad, then to Rashid, and finally back at Diana. "He said that he knew what it was like to want to die."

"It's got to be him," Diana said.

"And Frankie's out there with him." Cas bit her lip. "He doesn't know Z might be trying to set off another bomb."

The radio crackled, and the woman's voice said something about firefighters pulling another person out from the first floor. Then the sound faded. Rashid leaned closer, trying to hear the announcer as she talked about the identity of the first bomber, who . . . then there was nothing. The batteries had finally died.

"We have to warn Frankie." Diana tried to push Tad out of the path of the door.

Tad held his ground. "Stay here. Z and Frankie were going to go in opposite directions. If they did, then Frankie is most likely on the other side of the school from where the bomb will go off, and that's probably the safest place to be."

"What about us?" Cas asked, stepping toward Kaitlin.

"The bombs didn't destroy this area before," Rashid explained, trying to calm the panic growing inside him. The bomber might not be Z. If not, then it was someone else . . . maybe someone he was looking at now. "This room was the one least touched by the explosions."

"This room didn't get destroyed by those bombs," Diana said. "If the next explosion is above or below us, we won't be that lucky."

Cas shook her head.

"That's not going to happen," Tad insisted.

"How do *you* know?" Cas asked. "Why were you in the school anyway?"

Tad stared at her. "Didn't you just say the bomber was Z? Why question me?"

"I want to know why you were here. Do you have a reason?"

"Yeah. I had a reason." Tad looked toward the open doorway. "I got involved with someone this summer who I thought really liked me and I liked him, only he decided to stop answering my texts and my calls. I knew he'd be here today. I wanted him to have to face me instead of pretending like I didn't exist. I wanted him to have to look me in the eyes, because I'm tired of people not looking at me so they can pretend that I'm what they want me to be instead of facing who I really am." Tad spat out the last angry words. "I wanted him to know what it felt like to be me."

Rashid felt that anger down to his soul. He knew it better than he knew anything else in his life. He was Muslim. He was American. Most people seemed to think he couldn't really be either by being both. Too American to be a true Muslim. Too religiously observant to be a real American. There was no right way to be both. But he was both. All he wanted was to be himself—whoever that was. He just wanted the freedom to find out. "So you were going to try to make him really see you —kind of like me shaving my beard."

Tad cocked his head to the side. "Yeah." He nodded, almost to himself. "Yeah." He turned toward Cas. "But just because I'm tired of people pretending I'm not gay or that I'm not more than just white or black or whatever doesn't mean I was looking to blow up the school and my ass along with it."

"Well, the cops say they're looking at one of us." Cas looked around the room at each of them. "It could be Z, but it could be someone else. How can we be sure who it is?"

"What about Frankie?" Tad asked, stepping toward her.

Cas went still. "What about him?"

"He got the coach to cancel practice. The rest of the team is at the lake, far away from all of this. Kind of convenient, don't you think?"

"You think Frankie set the bombs?" Cas asked. "No way."

"Why?" Rashid asked her, even though the answer was

obvious. Frankie wasn't Muslim like he was or different because
he was half black and gay like Tad. But Rashid knew from experience that Frankie wasn't the perfect guy he claimed to be.
He'd seen him high-five his friends after they called Rashid or
other kids names.

"Frankie saved me," Cas explained. "When I was trapped in
the art room, Frankie got me out. I would have died in the fire
if he hadn't helped get me out. He wouldn't do this. He heard
me playing clarinet and stopped to talk to me."

Rashid frowned. "When? After the explosion?"

"No," she said. "Before. I was in the music wing. I just
wanted to play one last time before —"

"Before you killed yourself?" Diana finished for her.

Rashid held his breath as Cas looked down at the floor and
nodded.

"You were going to kill yourself here at school?" Rashid
asked, wiping his forehead.

"And maybe you didn't want to die alone?" Diana said.
"That would make sense. It would explain why you'd come here
instead of going somewhere private. You wanted to belong, and
once you died in the explosion, everyone would talk about you
as part of a group." Diana hadn't moved from her spot near the
doorway, making it clear to Rashid that she didn't trust any of
them enough to stand near them.

"What?" Cas took a step back, pressing herself against the
desk behind her. "No. That doesn't make any sense."

Only, as much as Rashid didn't want to jump to any

conclusions, it sort of did. "Suicide bombers in Palestine almost always target other people when they die. The more bodies, the more important the story."

Cas shook her head. "No" she insisted. "That's not what happened."

"Then why do it here?" Tad demanded. "Tell us."

"Why?" Cas looked up at the ceiling and bit her lip. "Because this is the place that makes me feel the worst about myself. I was worried I wouldn't go through with it if I tried to do it anywhere else. I figured if I got nervous or started to have second thoughts, I could just look around and remember why I didn't want to live anymore. And . . ."

"And what?" Rashid asked.

"And maybe I was hoping . . ." She shook her head. "It's stupid, but even though I wanted to end it all, I was waiting for something to happen."

"Like what?"

She sighed. "I don't know exactly. Something that would convince me things weren't all bad. That if I just waited for a few more days or weeks or even months, my life would get better. Frankie walking into my practice room and talking to me almost made me change my mind. If he'd come back again or if I'd talked to someone else, I might have taken my clarinet back and left. But the only other person I saw was Diana. I could tell you saw me, but you pretended you didn't and looked the other way."

"You can't blame me for you wanting to kill yourself," Diana snapped.

"She's not." Rashid wasn't sure that was accurate, but they didn't need more fighting. Not now, when Frankie and Z were out in the wreckage somewhere and one of them might be the bomber. And maybe trying to finish what he started . . . "We need to get out of here," he said. "Tad, help me get Kaitlin on the stretcher."

Tad grabbed one of the makeshift ropes and pulled on it. "These don't seem strong enough. They could break, and she'll drop to the cement. She'd die."

"She'll die if she stays here. The fire department has to have something they can put below so none of us hit the concrete. It's risky, but if Frankie or Z set off the next bomb—"

"The bomber isn't Frankie!" Cas yelled.

"It could be either of them. You saw Frankie downstairs in the music wing." Rashid turned to Cas. "Why would he be there? And did anyone see Z or Frankie anywhere else in the building before the explosions started?"

Cas shook her head.

Tad frowned. "I think I saw Kaitlin and Z through the window in the media center when I passed by, and the last time I saw Frankie was near the field house. Diana, did you . . . Diana?" Tad yelled, and Rashid turned toward the door where Diana had been standing.

"Where did she go?" Rashid hurried to the door and stepped

out into the corridor. Tad was right behind him. Side by side, they looked down the hall filled with broken beams and tiles and soot and destruction. But no Frankie or Z or Diana. She was gone.

"Guys!" Cas called from inside the room. Rashid ran back inside and looked at Kaitlin, expecting to see that she had stopped breathing, but her chest was still rising and falling.

"What's wrong?" he asked Cas, who was standing next to a table near the windows, staring into an unzipped blue bag. "Are you okay?"

She shook her head and looked up at him as Tad walked into the doorway. "I took a gun out of my grandfather's house and brought it with me to school today. I was going to use it to shoot myself."

For a moment, Rashid couldn't speak as he pictured the dark-haired girl with the olive skin and sad eyes pointing a gun at her head.

He could barely breathe as Cas tilted the bag and said, "The gun is gone."

FRANKIE

— CHAPTER 43 —

"**LEFT OR RIGHT?**" Frankie asked as he stepped over a broken two-by-four, coughed, and peered down the hallway. The left looked like the clearest path, but between his eyes adjusting from the classroom lit by sunlight and the dim, smoke-filled hall, it was hard to tell for certain.

Z looked in both directions and pointed to the right. "I'll shout if I find anything." Before Frankie could nod, Z leaped over a bunch of debris and bolted down the hallway. The guy was on a mission. So was Frankie. He needed to get out of here. Away from the fire and explosions and Tad.

Experimenting with Tad had been a mistake. He wasn't like Tad, Rashid, Cas, or Z. He wasn't looking for who he was supposed to be or trying to find people to accept him. Did he feel sorry for the others? Hell, yeah, but that didn't mean he had to make their choices. People liked him. He was a winner the way he was. Yeah, he needed to push boundaries every once in a while, but there were some boundaries he knew he couldn't cross without changing everything.

Something clanged behind him.

Heart jumping, he spun and squinted into the haze.

"Z?" he called.

Nothing. No Z. No crazy bomber dude or firefighter coming to save the day.

God, this all really sucked.

"Z?" he called again.

Still no answer.

Frankie turned and spotted a body covered in dust and debris next to a classroom door. The guy wasn't moving. Still, Frankie leaned down, felt for a pulse, and recognized the teacher staring lifelessly up at him.

Mr. Rizzo.

Frankie coughed. Bile burned up his throat. The taste of bitter metal and saliva flooded his mouth. *Nope.* He wasn't going to throw up. Although he could see he wouldn't be the first one to do so.

Kaitlin was near death. He was worried about dying himself. But the whole idea of dying still seemed unreal. Kind of like when Cas talked about killing herself. That seemed like something out of a story, not something that was really going to happen. Not like now. This was very real.

Shake it off, he could hear his father say. That's what a winner did. That's what anyone committed to a true purpose did. Shake it off and focus on doing what needed to be done. No doubts. Doubts only lead to hesitation, and hesitation to failure.

And failure here meant ending up like Mr. Rizzo or whoever else was buried under the rubble of the staircase that
Frankie was heading toward. Because he couldn't go back to the
room and wait there for whoever might come to save them. He
couldn't because that's not who he was supposed to be. He was
supposed to be the guy everyone admired, even though no one
could ever be all they expected him to be.

Frankie ducked under a bunch of wires to look at the mess
that used to be the stairs. Through the haze of smoke and the
dim light, he studied the wreckage. The stairs and the ceiling
and roof had caved in, making the prospects of getting down
this way slim. But when he looked down the hall that led to the
back of the school, it looked even worse. *Slim* was better than
nothing. Especially since Z wasn't calling out to say he'd found
a better way.

Glad to be doing anything other than sitting around in that
room, Frankie grabbed a board, yanked it out of the wreckage,
and threw it behind him. He yanked another out, then another,
and held his breath as debris moved and then settled. He was
reaching for another board when he heard voices. Not behind
him, where Diana and Tad and the others were waiting, but
somewhere . . . below. The voices were coming from below.

"Hello?" he called. "Is anyone there?"

Nothing. Then he heard the mumble of something . . .
someone yelling. It had to be the firefighters working to come
get them.

Yes. "Hey! We're up here."

Frankie heard something snap. He spun on his heel and almost barreled into Tad, who stumbled back, tripped over an iron bar, and slammed into an open locker with a crash.

"Sorry," Frankie said as Tad pushed himself upright. "I think there are rescue workers trying to come up through the stairs from below. I need to find Z and tell him."

"Wait." Tad grabbed his arm. "Have you seen Diana?"

"She's in the room with you."

"No." Tad shook his head. "One minute she was there, and the next, we all realized she'd disappeared. I was hoping she'd coming looking to warn you."

"Warn me about what?"

"They have a suspect in custody, and he said there's a second bomber and it's one of us."

Frankie turned back. "One of who?"

"Us," Tad said, pointing in the direction of the hallway they'd both come from. "With Z leaving and you going after him and with the cops thinking there's another bomb, we thought—"

"Wait a minute. You don't think I'm the bomber, do you?" Tad's hesitation kicked the air out of his chest. "Are you serious?" Frankie barely choked out. "Tad, you know me."

"I thought I knew you. I was wrong."

"And because I stopped answering your calls, you think I'm some kind of terrorist?"

"People do all sorts of crazy things when they don't like something about themselves. Cas was going to kill herself.

Rashid shaved off his beard. I wanted you to have to admit that what we had mattered. That all our talks and that kiss mattered."

Frankie glanced down the hall. "It was a mistake. I made a mistake."

Tad froze. Hurt flared in his deep brown eyes. "Good to know that's what I am to you. A mistake."

No. "That's not what I meant."

"I don't think you know what you meant, and it doesn't matter."

"Yes, it does. But you have to understand—"

"Understand what? That we're alike when we wear the same uniform and play on the same field, but beyond that, you want to be different from me? Trust me, I get it. I would have gotten it had you picked up the phone and given me the respect to tell me instead of just wishing I'd stay in the corner you shoved me into."

"That wasn't what I was doing." Wasn't it, though? Wasn't that exactly what he'd wanted? To make it all seem as if it never happened? To make himself believe it?

"Sure. Then why did you look like you were going to flip out when I showed up outside the field house? Everyone else went to the lake—captain's orders—but you were here. Why?"

"Well, it wasn't because I wanted to blow up the school. I was welcoming the freshman team and adding a few decorative touches around the school that I knew I could get away with. You wouldn't understand. You're—"

"Not important?" Tad shot back.

"Not *me*." Tad was just a guy on the field who didn't say much or get in anyone's way. Frankie won games and was a *leader*. He was perfect, even when he went out of his way to show everyone that he wasn't. His parents and Coach and everyone else would never learn, because they didn't want to learn. They didn't want him to be anything other than what they needed. Tad got to be whatever the hell he wanted, and still Tad thought he was trapped. Tad didn't know what trapped was. Or how hard it was to want to be the hero, even when you wanted nothing more than to crash and burn and break free.

"You're right." Tad nodded. "I'm not you, because I actually give a crap about other people, and right now I have to find Diana before she gets shot."

"Shot?" Frankie asked as Tad turned his back on him and headed down the hall in the direction they'd come from. "What the hell does that mean?"

A smoking beam fell from above. The floor beneath him shuddered when it smashed to the tile.

Tad stumbled. Frankie grabbed on to a splintered door frame and looked down at the ground that was still again. But if the building was too unstable to stand from all the bombs and the fire, how long until something else collapsed?

"Why would Diana get shot?" he asked.

Tad turned back. "There's a gun."

Everything stopped. "A gun? Why would there be a gun?"

"Cas brought it to the school."

To kill herself.

Despite what she'd said, Frankie hadn't really believed her when she'd admitted that she wanted to die. He hadn't wanted to believe her. He'd talked to her right before she went upstairs. He would have seen. He should have seen.

"The gun is loaded, and we think Z could have taken it. He told Cas he understood wanting to die."

Oh, hell. Hell! Frankie looked down the hall and tried to decide which play to call. He always knew. He never doubted. He called the shot. He ran the ball or put it in the air. No second-guessing. Second-guessing was for losers. Only right now, he wasn't sure what winning looked like.

Sweat trickled down Frankie's back. Something crackled from the stairwell. People were coming to save them, but if Z had a gun and knew where another bomb was, the rescue workers weren't going to make it in time.

"We have to find Z," Frankie said. "Maybe we can talk him out of whatever it is he's planning to do next." It was a long shot, but at this point it was a shot, and sometimes you had to make the Hail Mary play.

"Are you crazy?" Tad asked. "If he wants to blow the rest of this place up, we aren't going to be able to stop him. We have to—"

The air cracked.

A gunshot.

"Diana!" Frankie yelled, and bolted down the hall in the direction that Z had gone. He heard Cas's and Rashid's voices as he reached the room they were in. He grabbed the door frame and saw them carrying Kaitlin to the window on the stretcher they made.

Rashid spotted them and said, "The firefighters are setting up an inflatable cushion."

"Tad, you should stay and help them," Frankie said. "I'll go after Z and Diana."

Tad shook his head. "I'm not letting you go alone."

"Cas and I can do it," Rashid said, looking down at whatever was happening below. "Make sure no one else gets hurt."

Frankie would try.

As Rashid yelled for Cas to fasten the ropes to the legs of a desk, Frankie turned and bolted down the hall. Tad raced next to him. They reached the corner together.

Smoke. Far down the hallway. It was thicker. Black. Coming toward them.

Another crack.

"Diana!" Tad yelled.

Frankie winced, knowing that if Diana was in trouble, she wouldn't be the only one who could hear Tad yelling and the two of them approaching.

The cloud of dark smoke grew denser as they ran down the hall, which was streaked with soot and slick with water. With each step, Frankie waited to see Z appear or to hear Diana scream, but there was only smoke and debris and the sound of their footsteps as they raced through the hall that was pulsing with heat. Frankie rounded the corner right behind Tad, and another shot made him jump. He lost his footing, slipped, and crashed to the floor.

Oh, God. He yelped as something punched into his thigh.

"Frankie!" Tad called.

Pain flashed white in front of his eyes and up through his leg.

He bit his lip as he reached down and grabbed hold of the thin, metal spike protruding from his leg. "I'm okay." Not even close, but he could handle it. He had to handle it.

Tad yelled, "Stay down!"

Not if he could help it. Frankie tightened his grip on the metal bar as someone down the hall shouted, "Stop!"

Z.

Frankie's ears rang. Someone screamed. Frankie squinted into the haze.

"Get back," he heard Diana call out.

"What are you doing?" Z yelled. "Are you crazy? Don't do it."

There was the crack of another shot. Someone screamed, and through the smoke, Frankie saw a shadow crumple to the ground.

Tad?

Diana?

Frankie tightened his grip, closed his eyes, and counted — *one, two, three. Pull.*

Pain swelled. Blood pulsed, and he gritted his teeth as the

metal bar slid free. Tossing it to the side, he put a hand wet with blood onto the wall and got to his feet.

"Stay away from me!" Diana screamed.

"What are you doing?" Tad yelled back.

The world swirled, then steadied as Frankie balanced his weight on his good leg and peered through the thickening smoke. Sweat ran down his check. He spotted Tad standing beyond the entrance to what used to be the stairwell. He coughed, clenched his jaw against the agony in his leg, and limped forward, trying to see Diana and Z in the haze.

"You don't need to do this." Tad held his hands out and slowly crouched down near a classroom doorway. That's when Frankie saw Z lying on the floor and Diana standing across the hall from the two of them, a red backpack dangling from one hand as she stood still as a statue.

"What's going on?" Frankie asked.

Something crashed somewhere behind him. He started to glance over his shoulder when Diana swung her attention to him, and that's when he saw it.

Diana was the one with the gun.

2:01 P.M.

DIANA

– CHAPTER 44 –

"STAY BACK, FRANKIE," Diana ordered. Her heart pounded in her ears. This wasn't the way things were supposed to go. Nothing had gone the way it was supposed to go, and now she had no choice but to finish what she had started. It was the only way.

Still, she moved her feet and then the gun so that it was pointed at the football captain and all-around hero of the school. He didn't look anything like the guy she had once kissed as he limped a step toward her. The torn, dirty shorts. Hair coated in dust and debris and plastered down with sweat. Blood streaking down his leg.

Not so perfect now. Neither was she.

Smoke and dust billowed behind him.

Out of the corner of her eye, she saw something move, and she swung the gun back toward Tad, who had inched toward her. "Don't make me shoot you," she said. Not until she got closer. She'd never fired a gun before today. She'd almost dropped it when she had fired the first time. She could still feel the jolt. Still hear the shot. She'd missed on the second, but she hadn't missed the next time. Z was still alive, though.

Nothing was going as planned.

"What the hell do you think you're doing?" Z shouted. "Why the hell do you have a gun?"

"She thinks you're one of the bombers," Frankie said from behind her, and she angled so she could look back and forth among all three boys facing her, even as she wanted to scream.

They still didn't see *her*. They still didn't have a clue. They saw only what everyone saw, because it was all they wanted her to be—the popular girl from a wealthy, influential family. The one who smiled and followed the rules because that was the only thing her father needed from her.

But she needed more. She wanted to be more than that. And she'd figured out a way to do just that. Only now it was all falling apart. And even as she stood here in front of Tad and Frankie and Z, finally showing people that she wasn't the perfect girl and that she was capable of doing more, they still didn't see *her*.

Something cracked and crashed to the ground. The others jumped. Diana laughed. She couldn't help it. She had a gun, for God's sake. She had known why the first responders weren't coming into the building before anyone else. She understood why the bomb was set off when the firefighters came in and why someone would want to wait to set off another. "Don't you get it?" she asked. "It's *me*. I helped build the bombs. I brought them into the school. I'm the one behind all this."

It felt so good to finally say it. God, it was wonderful to tell someone other than Tim what she was capable of.

"You?" Z yelled as he struggled to get to his feet. Blood oozed through the fingers that he had clamped over his arm where she'd shot him.

Tad shook his head. "That doesn't make any sense."

Of course it didn't. Because Diana, with her practiced smiles, wouldn't do anything like this.

"Why? Because you think you know me?" she asked Tad. How could he know her when she wasn't even allowed to know herself? She looked at Frankie, who had limped another step forward. "How about you, Frankie? We've gone to school together for years. We dated until you backed off. Did you figure out I was smart enough to do this?"

"It isn't about being smart," Frankie insisted.

"Sure it is," she said, wiping the sweat dripping down her cheek onto the shoulder of her shirt, trying to keep her hands and the gun steady—like she'd been able to do when she and Tim were putting the gunpowder in the pipes. Slowly. Carefully. Checking to make sure there was no stray gunpowder on the top of the pipe when she closed it. Otherwise, one spark and—

"I'm smart enough to realize that my father needed help and that I could help him. Only he didn't want to let me work with his staff, because I'm just his daughter. To him, I'm only supposed to look perfect and smile at the camera. But I know I can do more, so I came up with my own plan. How many people who opposed the Safety Through Education bill will decide it's necessary after today? Just look at how dangerous schools can be. We need to do more to help empower teachers and students to keep the country safe."

"You blew up the school so your father could pass his stupid bill?"

She leveled the gun at Z, who looked at her with narrow eyes. He thought he understood her. He didn't. Not like Tim. Her father's aide understood that sometimes being a patriot meant using any means necessary to persuade people to follow the right path. She'd only had to say how the hate mail she was receiving made her want to go blow something up to prove to people how necessary the bill was to catch Tim's attention. "People don't always understand why something is necessary until you show them."

"So you blew up the school with you inside it to prove your father's point?" Frankie asked.

"I wasn't supposed to be inside," she snapped. The first explosions were supposed to be set off two hours later—when the yearbook meeting was originally supposed to take place. The building should have been empty by then. She'd changed the meeting time to earlier so that her father and his staff could claim that she was the target and that she escaped only because of the last-minute scheduling adjustment. But something had gone wrong. She'd done everything exactly the way she and Tim had planned, and still, here she was. And Tim had been caught, and now . . . now they would know it was her. She wouldn't be standing at her father's side, telling everyone how she believed his bill would have helped prevent the destruction. Tim wouldn't be around to direct the press toward the evidence he'd planted that was supposed to point at one of the students who had previously been suspended for making threats. Diana had even suggested it should be Z, because he was never in school. And he was here. She'd actually thought that maybe Tim had figured out a way to get him here. But that wasn't the case.

She thought Tim must have screwed up the timers. He was the one who had insisted on handling that part. The bombs were all supposed to go off later, and in three waves, to make people think that the person behind the attacks was somewhere near the school, setting them off with a cell phone. Tim and Diana were supposed to be far away from it all. No one was supposed to suspect them.

But maybe the timers hadn't been screwed up at all. Maybe Tim had wanted her to die so her father could cry and claim that his bill could have saved her life. She could see how he could make that work. Her father would become the brave senator who continued to work to make sure everyone else in the country could be protected the way his daughter had not been.

Everything she had planned was falling apart. She had to find a way to keep it together. But even if she shot Tad and Frankie and Z and then set off the bomb she had in the bag —the one that she had intended to leave near the entrance on her way out of the school so that it would go off with the others

—nothing would be as it was supposed to be. Her father would be ruined. He would never get reelected or be able to run for another office. Diana would face a trial. People had died. She hadn't wanted them to, but they had. She would be blamed. There would be a trial. She'd go to jail.

If she hadn't gotten caught in the blast . . .

If Tim hadn't gotten arrested . . .

If . . .

"So now what?" Z took a step toward her, and she swung the gun toward him. "You're going to kill us and then just waltz out of here, pretending none of this ever happened?"

When she'd left the classroom, she'd set the timer for fifteen minutes. She was going to finish what she'd started.

Smoke billowed down the hall.

"Diana." Frankie looked down at the gun and then back at her face, "you don't have to do this."

Yes. She did. She had done what she believed had to be done —what Tim told her that her father secretly wished would happen. Yet somehow she'd ruined it all. Her father's career. Her life. And there was no going back from that.

People see what you want them to see.

And she hadn't really wanted to help her father, no matter how much she'd told herself she did. She had just wanted him to realize what could have happened had she been in the building when the bomb went off. She just wanted him to see her. Only things had gone wrong. She was trapped in the building. And now everyone would see who she was.

She straightened her shoulders and tightened her grip on the gun and fired.

Diana stumbled back. Her ears rang. Tad's eyes opened wide as the bullet bit into him.

"Tad," Frankie cried, hobbling forward.

Diana swung the gun toward Frankie as Tad grabbed his stomach. Blood oozed over his fingers. His mouth opened with surprise as he sank to the ground.

She couldn't breathe as she clutched the gun tighter in her sweat-slick hands and altered her stance to point it at Z, who was leaning over Tad, telling him everything was going to be okay. That he was going to be okay.

Nothing was going to be okay. Not for her. Not for anyone, she thought as Rashid burst through the smoke.

"The firefighters have an air cushion down below. We lowered Kaitlin down and Cas—" Rashid stopped twenty feet away and lifted his eyes to meet hers. "You?"

She didn't bother to nod. She just stood there with the gun raised. Her heart pounding.

"We can all leave," Rashid said calmly, taking a step forward. "It's over."

He was right. It was over.

But Diana didn't drop the gun. Because it couldn't be over. Not for her.

2:05 P.M.

RASHID

— CHAPTER 45 —

WHAT SHOULD HE DO? Rashid kept his eyes focused on the gun in Diana's hands. He had no idea what to do. Frankie was favoring one leg. Z was leaning over Tad, who was coughing and clutching his bloody stomach. And Diana's eyes were narrowed and her face tense with concentration as she prepared to shoot again.

Something crashed behind him. Sweat ran down his back. After Frankie had yelled that he and Tad were going after Diana and Z, Rashid had made sure the ropes they'd made were tied as securely as possible to the legs on a desk near the window. He had Cas yell to the firefighters that they were sending an injured girl down and with her help got the stretcher and Kaitlin out the window.

At first, he hadn't been able to breathe as he slowly eased Kaitlin down a few inches at a time, but the ropes held. Cas lost control of the side she'd been lowering, but Kaitlin had been far down enough for the firefighters to catch her. She was in their hands now. So was Cas. She hadn't thought she could make it through the window or jump to the cushion below, but she'd done both. As soon as he saw her safely hit the yellow inflated mattress and the firefighters reach for her, Rashid had run out of the room to find Tad and the others. He could have jumped too. He'd told Cas he would, but not yet. If Z was the bomber, maybe learning that Kaitlin was with the paramedics would stop him from whatever he was going to do. If not —well, Rashid couldn't leave Tad and Frankie to die, knowing he might be able to save them.

The temperature had grown hotter with every step as he'd hurried around the wreckage and down the hall. The tiles above this floor were blistered as he raced through. The ceiling looked as if it could come down at any second. If another bomb did go off—

"Rashid." Frankie looked over his shoulder at him. His face was tense with pain and fear. "Get out of here."

Blood dripped down Frankie's leg. He looked ready to drop.

"Don't move," Diana called. The gun pointed at Frankie swung toward Rashid. Diana's voice was firm and in control, but the way the gun shook in her hands told a different story. Rashid focused on that and not on the way the barrel was leveled at him or how hard it was for him to catch his breath.

"Go, Rashid." Z yelled. "Run!"

"No one is going anywhere!" Diana took a step forward and glanced down at Tad.

Rashid watched Diana's eyes rise and flick back and forth from person to person, as if she wasn't sure what to do. And even though he wanted to run—everything inside him screamed to flee—he stepped forward so that he was standing shoulder to shoulder with Frankie.

"What are you doing?" Frankie hissed. "She has a bomb. In that bag, there's a bomb."

Rashid swallowed hard but held his ground.

"Stay where you are!" Diana shouted. "One more step, and I'll shoot."

She might. She'd shot Tad. She could shoot him. Rashid didn't want to die, but he moved in front of the football quarterback. And no shot was fired.

Diana backed up against the wall. The gun was now aimed at Rashid. The bag in Diana's hand dangled just above the ground.

"Get out of here, Frankie," Rashid said, then held his breath and took another step forward.

If the bomb went off, all of them would get caught in the blast. Frankie and the others weren't going to be able to move quickly. Tad had been shot. He was losing blood fast and needed help. Z did too. Frankie couldn't move very fast. He might not be able to stand much longer on that leg. And Z couldn't carry Tad—not with his injured arm. Rashid needed to buy them time to get away. If they could get around the corner, he'd run. He really wanted to run.

Rashid glanced at Frankie, then at Z. "Get out of here. I'll be right behind you," he said quietly, stepping forward yet again as Diana followed his movements with the gun. But his eyes were on the red backpack dangling from her hand. Would the bomb inside go off if she dropped it? *Please don't let it go off.*

His eyes watered. His throat burned. Still, he kept his eyes focused on Diana and moved forward again, closing the space between them, keeping her attention on him.

The gun.

The bag and the bomb.

The trembling girl.

He had never been so scared.

Sweat dripped down his forehead.

The gun was only ten feet away from him. Close enough for her to hit what she aimed for. If she fired, he would die. If he rushed at her and she dropped the bag, he could die.

"You can let them go. They don't need to die, Diana. You already got what you wanted," he said, hoping that was true.

Behind the gun, she was breathing hard. Her back was pressed to the wall. Her eyes flicked from person to person before resting on the bag.

"Let them go, Diana. Killing them won't change anything. Letting them live will, though."

Her eyes flicked to him. "How?"

He glanced down at Tad, lying on the floor. His breathing was shallow. His eyes were wide with fear and shock.

"Think about it," he said. "You understand how this works better than anyone. Everybody will want to hear their story, and every time they tell it, people will talk about what you did here." Keeping his eyes on Diana, he waved his hand behind him and quietly said, "Z, Frankie, I'll get Tad. It's time for the two of you to get out of here. Go now."

He heard the guys scramble. Frankie swore. Rashid could hear them moving, but he couldn't look back to see how fast they were going. He had to keep her attention. Just for a few seconds. Diana looked as if she was going to shoot, then dropped the barrel of the gun just an inch. Enough to let him know she didn't want to fire but there was still the bag and the bomb inside it.

"I don't believe you wanted to kill people with these bombs," he told her, hoping it was true. He had seen the way her face drained of color each time she had looked at Kaitlin. The horror she had felt was real. It had to have been.

She shook her head. "The first bomb was supposed to go off later. Everyone should have been out of the building by then. It was a mistake. It had to be a mistake." She shook her head. "That doesn't matter now. None of it matters."

"It all matters," he said. "And it means you don't want to do this. You don't want to kill them. I don't think you want to kill me."

Diana held up the red backpack. "I set the timer. This bomb is going to go off."

Don't panic. Keep calm. No fear.

"I don't know you," he said. He heard footsteps going down the hall and wanted to look to see where they were, but he had to focus on Diana. Just a few more seconds so the others could get around the corner, where they'd have some protection from a blast. "I've never spoken to you until today," he said, trying to find something to say. Anything. "I've never really thought about you, and I don't think you've ever really thought about me. Have you?"

"Have I what?" Diana blinked and tilted her head as she studied him over the gun.

"Have you thought about me?" he asked, edging a little closer.

She barely moved as she looked at him with glassy eyes. "No."

"None of your friends made fun of my clothes or my beard or whispered about me when I came down the hall?"

"Do you want an apology?" Diana asked dully.

"What I want is to get out of here without anyone else getting hurt. This has to end." *No more fire or fear.*

"To end . . ." Diana shook her head. "This isn't the way it was supposed to end. I just wanted for my father to see . . ."

"Your father would want you to stop the bomb." He took a deep breath and wiped his palms on his pant legs. "You don't have to do this anymore." Desperation twisted Diana's face. Rashid took a step closer so the bag with the bomb was only a few steps away. If he could get it, maybe he could stop the timer or put it somewhere it would cause the least amount of damage. "I don't know what your life is like. I only know what it looks like. But I know you don't have to do this. You can walk out of here with us."

She frowned. Tears glistened in her eyes. One ran down her

face as she looked from Rashid down to Tad. "No, I can't. This was my one chance."

"We all have lots of chances. Look at Cas. She thought her chance was over, but now she gets another one. You can have another one too. You just have to stop the bomb and help me get Tad out of here. You're strong enough to do this."

The gun in Diana's hand shook. She looked back at Tad and then up at Rashid. "You're wrong about what my father would want. He'll be better off if I'm dead. And even if that wasn't true, I'm not that strong." She walked backwards down the hall away from him, her eyes now clear and free of tears. The bag tight in one hand. The gun in the other. "You'd better hurry. You only have a few minutes before the bomb goes off." Her voice was flat. Calm. Terrifying. "Tell Cas you were right. It does take courage."

"Diana . . ."

"If you want to live, you have to go," she said as she stepped under a fallen board and disappeared from sight.

Move, he told himself, *now.*

He snaked his arms under Tad's armpits and pulled. Tad's tortured groan made Rashid's knees go weak, but he kept pulling. Two feet. Six. Ten. Blood streaking their path. Tad's blood. He wasn't going to make it at this rate.

Rashid's heart hammered hard as he pulled Tad down the hall. How long did they have before the bomb went off? Rashid glanced over his shoulder. He was almost to the end of the hallway. He had to get around the corner. Just a few more feet. *Please let me make it just a few more feet.*

Tad screamed. Rashid screamed too as he leaned back and pulled as hard as he could until they finally reached the end of the hallway. He looked back into the haze, trying to see Diana. For a second, he thought he saw a shadow before he dragged Tad again and rounded the corner.

He pulled Tad into the closest classroom and slammed the door shut.

As the explosion rocked behind him, he pictured Diana's beautiful face. Hers was the face of a girl who looked happy. She looked as if she had every reason to live. But under it all, she was a bomb with a fuse that had been lit and was waiting to explode.

"We're okay, Tad," he said as he heard shouting down the hall. Firefighters had finally arrived. "It's over."

The greatest trap in our life is not success, popularity, or power, but self-rejection.

—Henri Nouwen

FIVE WEEKS LATER . . .

CAS

– CHAPTER 46 –

WHY?

Cas looked out the window as her mother pulled into the student parking lot that had looked so far away from the second-story classroom window more than a month ago.

All because Diana wanted to prove that her father's bill was necessary. At least, that's what everyone said. The senator's aide who planned the bombing with Diana had told the authorities that it had been her idea to demonstrate how vital the Safety Through Education law was. But it had done the opposite, because not one person could think of anything that had indicated Diana was planning something like this. Diana was the last student anyone would have reported to the administration, and yet she was the time bomb that had been waiting to go off.

Rashid and Frankie and Z had told the FBI and the cops and everyone else who interviewed them what she had said before letting them all leave and setting off the final bomb. She'd never meant to get caught in the blast and had believed her father's aide had set up another student to take the fall. On the advice of his lawyer, the senator's aide wasn't talking anymore, but everyone was speculating that he had always intended for Diana to die. A senator losing a daughter to the kind of violence his bill was trying to prevent was far more sympathetic than one whose daughter had lived. The aide said he and Diana had been working for the greater good. Maybe he even believed it. After talking to Rashid, Cas wasn't sure what Diana had believed.

"Are you sure you don't want me to pick you up later?" Cas's mom asked.

"Rashid said he'd drive me home," she said, looking at the construction crews sweating in the September sun. It was hot today, but that didn't matter to Cas as she opened the SUV door and hopped out of the car. "I'm okay, Mom. Really. It's not like there's any reason for someone to blow this place up again," she said as she straightened her black tank and black shorts. Her mother gave her an uncertain smile. Cas was getting that smile a lot nowadays, but it was better than the manic one that tried to pretend everything was normal.

Waving to her mom, Cas turned and looked at the building sitting on the hill that was slowly being put back together. It would be months before it was back to normal. As if that was possible.

The administration was saying that the school would partially reopen in January. No one she knew actually thought the damage could be fixed so fast, but Cas hoped it would be. She wanted to believe that mending what was broken could be done quickly if you wanted it badly enough. But until the school was ready, classes and all activities were being held at the community college. Cas's mother, her father, even her new but still annoying shrink assumed that after everything, she would want to attend a different school or be homeschooled. Homeschooling would mean no kids to face. No repercussions for the rules she'd broken. She could just forget that it and everything else she was running from had ever happened.

Only she didn't want to forget.

She spotted Tad coming out of a group of trees. His eyes were firmly fixed on the building where their lives had changed, so he didn't see her watching him—studying how gingerly he was walking. She'd been in the hospital for two days with the blood loss and risk of infection. He'd been in for more than a week. All because of the gun she'd brought with her.

The gun.

Explaining it—how it had gotten into Diana's hands and why Cas had brought it to the school in the first place—was the hardest thing she'd ever had to do.

Seeing her father's expression.

Watching her mother cry.

The hundred hours of community service she had been given for her actions were nothing compared to the way people pretended not to stare when she walked by. They all now knew that Cas had gone into the school that day intending to die.

But fate had intervened, and Cas was alive.

She saw Tad turn toward her. The haunted, hollow look

she'd seen when he had first woken up from surgery was still there. Cas wondered if it would ever fade.

Rashid had given her a message from Diana. Cas hadn't been sure she wanted to hear it, but it was hard to ignore someone's final words, even if that someone had called you a coward. Cas thought about those words now as she watched Tad checking his phone and walked to meet him.

Rashid was right.

When Cas had admitted to everyone that she'd wanted to die, Rashid had said it took courage to live.

Yeah. It did.

TAD

— CHAPTER 47 —

"**FRANKIE'S NOT COMING,**" Tad called to Cas as she walked toward him. She looked different. Her dark hair was shorter and had some kind of blond highlights that, against the brown and with the black eyeliner she was wearing, made her look harder . . . but in a good way. Or maybe it was the way she studied the building behind him that made her seem so different. As if she was determined not to let it beat her.

Tad felt the same. It's why he sat in the stands of every practice, even though he wasn't cleared by the doctors to play. Some of the guys had transferred to other schools. Frankie had. Now one of the junior varsity quarterbacks was leading the team, and Frankie didn't seem to mind. The two of them had talked a couple of times since it happened. Tad had insisted and hadn't let Frankie dodge him. He was done with being pushed aside. Tad told Frankie he needed him to listen. And Frankie had. The conversations weren't easy or comfortable . . . not like the ones they'd had in July, when things were different between them. It was hard to watch someone you cared about pretend to be someone he wasn't. Or maybe he wasn't pretending. Tad had realized it wasn't up to him to decide that. Only Frankie could. All Tad could do was live his life the way he wanted to. He wasn't sure what that meant yet, but he'd figure it out.

Tad put his hand on his abdomen where they'd removed the bullet. The ache would eventually fade, but he wondered if it would ever go away. The upside was that if he ever decided to go into acting, he'd be able to play a guy who got blown up and shot and look as if he knew what he was doing.

One day at a time, his father had said when Tad got out of the hospital. Tad was trying, but, really, it all still sucked.

"Did Frankie say why he's not coming?" Cas asked Tad as she stopped next to him.

He held out his phone so Cas could read the text.

CELEBRATING YESTERDAY'S WIN WITH SOME OF THE NEW TEAM. TELL EVERYONE I SAY HELLO.

Frankie had bailed on them, but he'd sent a message. For Frankie, that was progress.

No one was surprised when Frankie and his sister enrolled in a different school or how now that Frankie was healed, he was leading a new team to victory. If he wanted to be noticed by scouts for a football scholarship, every game counted. So far, Frankie's new school had won every game. Tad's squad couldn't say the same. Frankie's new team had beaten them soundly last night.

"He played a good game," Cas said. Tad shrugged. Cas had come to the game and sat with Tad as he watched Frankie connect with his new receiver. He hadn't told Cas to come. She had just slid into the seat next to him and asked him to explain what she was watching while the crowd seated on both sides of the field cheered for Frankie's return. Even when he was playing against them, people viewed Frankie as a hero.

"You should have hung out with your team after the game," Cas said. "You need to be with your friends."

"I might next week," said Tad, not sure if he would. "Or maybe I'll skip the game and watch a bad horror movie instead."

Cas smiled. "Either way, you'll see a slaughter."

Tad smiled back. "Except one comes with a more comfortable chair." At this point, that sounded pretty good to him. "So when are we going to do this thing?"

"Rashid's waiting at the Park," she said, looking at her phone.

"Then let's go find him." It was time to do what they came here to do.

FRANKIE

– CHAPTER 48 –

HE WATCHED THEM from the street. Cas and Tad looking up at the school. The two of them walking off to meet Rashid at the spot everyone called the Park. Browning grass and a couple of trees wasn't exactly his idea of a park. But people liked labels to tell them what to think.

Hell, they had labeled him a hero. All the talk shows wanted him to speak about Diana and surviving the bombing. Someone even offered to represent him if he wanted to write a book. His father said he should think about it—after all, Frankie *had* saved Cas's life and he'd dated Diana, so he had insight into what people on TV were calling her complicated mind. But all Frankie wanted to do was pretend none of it had ever happened. That nothing that occurred this summer had ever happened.

It was over. He was at a different school now, with different friends. No one knew about why Tad had been in the school when Diana had tried to blow them up. All people knew was that she'd done something crazy to help her father and that she was dead. Kaitlin was too.

Frankie could still see Kaitlin's pale face and hear the way she told Z it was all going to be okay, even though her legs were crushed. She had to know she was going to die. Yet no one was calling *her* a hero. That just showed how stupid the world was. Everyone saw what they wanted to see. Kaitlin was a victim. She was dead, and heroes didn't die. Heroes saved the girl when they saved the day.

Technically, Z should have been a hero as well, but no one knew where to find him. One day he was in the hospital and talking to all the cops and FBI agents like the rest of them; the next he was gone. Frankie had heard Z wasn't attending classes at the community college and no one at the other schools where students had enrolled had run into him. Rashid claimed Z had headed for California, but no one else had heard from Z. No one knew what to believe. It had almost become a game online to speculate where Z had gone and what he had been doing in the school in the first place. Yet, despite varsity practice being canceled, no one ever questioned why Frankie had been there.

He looked back at the building and wondered if any of his handiwork had survived the fires. The one in the field house had been his best effort, and it was the part of the school with the least damage. He was pretty sure someone must have seen the tag line Frankie had added under the HOME OF THE TROJANS sign.

Because a good offense starts with a great defense.

Of course, if anyone had noticed, no one cared about who might be responsible. The high school got blown up. More than a dozen people died. And his parents' first priority after all that had happened was to get him into a new school so he could make the most of his senior year. They still needed him to get over the bar and win. To still be the guy that everyone looked up to. And winners didn't go off track. They didn't think about the things that could upset everything. They looked for the next challenge and didn't look back. Not even when they wished they could. *Maybe someday,* he thought. *But not yet. Not now.*

Frankie spotted Rashid walking down the sidewalk toward the Park, where Cas and Tad were waiting—one who thought he was a hero, and the other who knew he wasn't.

Rashid disappeared behind a tree, and Frankie put the car in gear and drove away.

No looking back. Because that's who he was.

RASHID

— CHAPTER 49 —

RASHID LOOKED AT THE SCHOOL. It was amazing how fast brick and mortar that had appeared so sturdy could be taken apart and how quickly the process of putting it together again began. It already looked very different from that day when firefighters led him to safety.

He understood the need to wipe away the signs of the destruction Diana had caused. To pretend that things hadn't gone off the rails and that everything was just fine now that the threat was gone.

Rashid shook his head, adjusted the bag on his shoulder, and walked across the grass that crunched under his feet. Rain was in the forecast for tonight, his father said. Then things would turn green again.

His father claimed he wasn't angry that Rashid had shaved. *Disappointed* was the right word. Rashid still wasn't sure if it was disappointment that Rashid hadn't talked to him about it or that he had done it in the first place. But he was grateful when his father said Rashid could choose whether or not to keep shaving, even when it was clear his father wished for him to stop. "What is good for one man is not the right choice for another."

Right now, letting his beard grow back was the right choice for Rashid. After everything that he'd gone through in order to blend in, it was funny that he no longer wanted to. When he'd called his sister after the first bomb went off, she hadn't answered. So he'd left a message telling her that he hoped she would always be true to herself and live the life she wanted to live. It was something he wished he had done more of before that day, and now he was trying to take his own advice. Shaving a beard wouldn't change how people thought of him. Not really. But talking to them about why he had the beard might. If nothing else, it was a place to start, and he'd go from there.

"Frankie bailed," Tad said as Rashid sat on the dry grass, grateful for the breeze and the shade of the tree.

"Did he say why?" Rashid asked.

"Team party."

Rashid wasn't surprised that Frankie hadn't come. He had looked uncomfortable when Rashid had talked to him in the hospital after the bombing and when Rashid had asked for his phone number.

"No matter what happens," Rashid had told him, "I'd like all of us to stay in touch. No one else will ever understand what it was like."

Which is why Rashid had invited Frankie today and why,

even though it would be easier without him, Rashid wished he were here.

"I told Tad he should party with his football friends too," Cas said. Rashid knew she was concerned about how much time Tad spent alone. It was part of the reason Rashid had asked them to meet.

"And I told Bossy that I'd consider it. Although I think maybe I've come up with a better idea for all of us next Friday." Tad looked at Rashid. "So maybe someone would like to tell us why we're at school on a Saturday?"

Rashid unzipped the backpack and pulled out three of the five small pieces of broken, charred tile he'd taken from the wreckage before they began reconstruction. "I thought you guys should have these and I thought this was the best place to give them to you."

Cas took the blackened tile Rashid held out to her and ran her finger over the jagged edge.

"Everyone keeps saying everything will be back to normal soon, but I want to remember," he said. *Remember. Forgive. Understand. All of it.*

It's why he had the photograph of the girl he'd found in the bathroom on his nightstand, along with pictures he'd copied from the yearbook of everyone who had been stuck in that room while the fire raged and bombs threatened. Z was actually smiling in his photograph. Something Rashid saw him do only once in person, when Rashid had walked into his hospital room after he'd come out of recovery. The bullet had been removed.

No permanent damage had been done. Rashid just wished that the other scars would heal as well.

"Hey," Z had said, sitting up against the pillows on the bed.

"I just wanted to come by and tell you how sorry I am." Kaitlin had died in surgery. They'd done their best, but it hadn't been good enough. It was amazing she had survived as long as she had. Z had shrugged and looked off toward the window while Rashid transferred his weight back and forth, trying to come up with something else to say. "You know, you still haven't told me why you're called Z."

"You really want to know?" Z had looked back at him. "When my mom was first diagnosed, she told me she was going to beat it, because she wanted to be there for me. So she was going to follow every step her doctors told her to take—*A* to *Z*. After that, I called myself Z to remind her I'd be there at the end of it all. Guess I need to go back to calling myself Alex now."

"I don't know," Rashid had said. "I kind of like Z. It suits you."

"Why?"

"Because you chose it."

When leaving the room, Rashid had turned back and for a second caught a glimpse of the smile from the photograph in the yearbook. The next day, there had been a note waiting for Rashid at the nurse's station.

GOING TO CALIFORNIA. THANKS FOR EVERYTHING. — Z

This time it had been Rashid who smiled, because Z had chosen who he wanted to be. And wasn't that what they were all trying to do?

Tad lifted the tile to his nose. "I'll never forget this smell."

"It smells like fear," Cas said.

Rashid looked at the two of them and said, "And courage."

"Kind of like going to high school." Tad laughed.

Cas smiled. "It would be nice if it would get easier."

"Yeah," Rashid said, looking back at the school where so much had happened. Where so much would continue to happen. *Yeah, it would.*

ACKNOWLEDGMENTS

There are people who make both your life and your work better. My life was improved in so many ways the moment my agent, Stacia Decker, decided to take a chance on me. Since that day she has believed in me even when I'm not sure I believe in myself. Stacia—thank you from the bottom of my heart for being my friend, my champion, and a voice of reason when I need it most. You make me a better writer and I'm lucky to have you on my side.

I'm also fortunate to have an amazing team who stands by me and makes everything I do look better than I ever could have imagined. First and foremost, Margaret Raymo, who always trusts that I will take thoughtful comments and turn them into something that shines. Karen Walsh and Lauren Cepero, PR extraordinaires, who field my crazy emails with grace and friendship. Ali Schmelzle, the most amazing cheerleader a girl could have in addition to being a sales expert. And to Mary Wilcox, Linda Magram, Candace Finn, Lisa DiSarro, and so many others who have gone above and beyond to take my words and put them into the hands of readers—thank you from the bottom of my heart. Also, to Catherine Onder, HMH Books for Young Readers' fearless leader and publisher, thank you for your vision and leadership.

All stories are personal, but this one forced me to look at life in a very different way and to walk in shoes that are not my own. Thank you to all of the students, teachers, and friends who were willing to talk to me about their lives and to help me see the world through new lenses. I owe a very special thanks to Tayaba Inam, Ann Carboneau, Becca Hix, Kimmily Phan, Yokabit Ayele, Malik Basham, Brittany Bush, Maria Celeste Hernandez, Thomas Holmes, Aja Martin, and Jennifer Weaver for your point of view on this story and for helping me make the characters as real as I could.

Thanks also to my mother, Jaci, for your never-ending well of support. Also, my deepest love and gratitude go to my husband and son, who gave me the space I needed to write and rewrite this book (which wasn't easy to find in the middle of a house remodel) until it was something I could be proud of.

I owe a large group hug to everyone at the Dunow, Carlson, and Lerner Literary Agency and to Sean Daily of Hotchkiss and Associates for your support.

And finally, to all the teachers and librarians and readers and booksellers who have welcomed my books into their hearts—none of the words I write would matter if it wasn't for you.